From the Heart

Coleen Murtagh Paratore is the author of several books for young readers, including her debut novel *The Wedding Planner's Daughter*, which launched a bestselling series. The mother of three handsome teenage sons, Coleen lives in Albany, New York, and loves inspiring others and sharing the joy of writing with audiences of all ages.

D0168568

Also by Coleen Murtagh Paratore

The Wedding Planner's Daughter
The Wedding Planner's Daughter: Playing Cupid
The Wedding Planner's Daughter:
Star-Crossed Summer

The Wedding Planner's Daughter

From the Heart

Coleen Murtagh Paratore

MACMILLAN CHILDREN'S BOOKS

First published in the USA 2009 by Scholastic Press, an imprint of Scholastic Inc.

First published in the UK 2009 by Macmillan Children's Books
a division of Macmillan Publishers Limited
20 New Wharf Road, London N1 9RR
Basingstoke and Oxford
Associated companies throughout the world
www.panmacmillan.com

ISBN 978-0-330-45806-1

Copyright © Coleen Murtagh Paratore 2009

1 3 5 7 9 8 6 4 2

A CIP catalogue record for this book is available from
the British Library.

Typeset by Nigel Hazle
Printed and bound in the UK by CPI Mackays, Chatham ME5 8TD

To my 'most fun' friend,
Kathy Johnson.
– C. M. P.

Contents

1   Sea-Spired 1
2   'Greenzilla' 13
3   Sweet Rosie Sweets 19
4   Wild Rhymes 28
5   Sailing Lessons 36
6   No Mutts About It 46
7   Beauty and the Bites 57
8   Family Day 66
9   Beach Rights 74
10 Everyone's Writing Books 85
11 A Mermaid Gift 97
12 No Buts About It 102
13 Salty from the Sea 114
14 Stupid Baseball 124
15 Bad, Bad Bottle 137
16 The Cape Cod Beach Boys 149
17 Two Planets Colliding 157
18 Wave Talk 166
19 Kindred Spirits After All 175
20 Willa the Wedding Planner 182
21 A Startling Surprise on the Spit 190

Willa's Skinny-Punch Summer Pix 194

Sea-Spired

I wiped away the weeds and foam,
I fetched my sea-born treasures home;
But the poor, unsightly, noisome things
Had left their beauty on the shore,
With the sun and the sand and the wild uproar.

— Ralph Waldo Emerson

I open my journal and begin to write:

You must be brave to walk the beach alone. After all,
you are only human. You may be simply looking for
heart-shaped rocks or orange jingle shells, when, in
a blink, three giants – Air, Water and Earth – might
converge upon you to form Fire. Fired, inspired, sea-
spired, your heart speaks a language only you can
hear.

Suddenly your problem is solved, your path is clear, you have a wonderful idea! Lighter now, happier, your pace quickens as you turn home. The footprints you made only minutes ago are now part of the infinite sea.

A new you makes new prints in the sand, new marks upon the planet, dinosaur-sized next to the birds, the seagulls, terns and plovers.

The beach is never the same beach twice.

Blink and it changes.

Blink and it changes.

Blink and you are changed.

I stop writing, read it over, smile. Such grand thoughts by the sea, Willa.

I ruffle through my beach-bag for a water bottle. No luck. How could I have forgotten one? We have a whole fridge full at home. My mother ordered a hundred cases with our new green and gold 'Inn' logo: 'Only the best for Bramblebriar guests. Fresh from a mountain stream.'

It's eight thirty a.m. I still have some time before work. Leaving my bag, I walk out along the Spit, a long narrow stretch of beach with calm

Popponesset Bay on one side, the wide open Atlantic Ocean on the other. It's my favourite place in the world.

Three tiny birds, piping plovers they're called, white bellied, mottled brown and tan feathers, stick legs, just inches high, scurry along in front of me, peck, peck, pecking for breakfast crabs. *Good morning, plovers.*

When I reach the prettiest part of the Spit, there are workers hammering wooden stakes into the sand, stringing red ropes between them. They look over at me and I wave. Every summer about this time, the Massachusetts Audubon Society cordons off sections of the beach where the piping plovers and the terns, two types of endangered bird, are nesting. This year they're closing off an unusually large area of grade-A top-choice Bramble beach. People aren't going to like this at all.

Right now, the Spit is just sand and birds. By noon the boats will have landed and anchored and the beach will be covered with blankets, umbrellas, tables and chairs, grills, coolers, volleyball nets, toys and tons of people. Come the fourth of July, you won't be able to walk by the water without tripping over anchor lines.

Every summer there's always a bit of local nastiness about the endangered bird thing, because you can't bring dogs on the beach when the birds are nesting. Dogs might trample the birds' fragile eggs. Seagulls launch sinister aerial attacks, but you can't put a leash on a seagull. Some people ignore the rules and let their dogs run free. Other people call the hotline to snitch. It makes the papers for a day or two and then *poof* – it's over until next year. I don't pay too much attention. We don't have a dog. My mother says we aren't 'dog people'.

But this year the birds aren't just messing with dog-people fun. This summer they're messing with boat-people fun. Those fancy yacht owners will be angry about the birds taking over their favourite part of the beach. This could get interesting.

At the tip of the Spit I stop and head back the way I came. My throat is tight and achy now. I can't believe I forgot water. The waves lap loudly, taunting me. Water as far as my eyes can see. *Water, water, everywhere, Nor any drop to* . . .

'Willa!' My new friend, Mariel Sanchez, is coming up over the dune. Dripping wet, out of breath, she hurries towards me carrying something. Mare is an early bird beach-girl too. I walk; she swims, way out by the buoys. I would never swim out that far. I have my reasons. A nasty run-in with a jellyfish when I was younger. It seems silly to still be afraid; it happened so long ago. And then there is the memory of how my birth father died at sea . . .

'Look what the tide brought in,' Mare says.

It's a black rubber snorkel with goggles attached, all tangled up in slimy seaweed.

'That's cool, Mare.'

'I've always wanted to snorkel,' she says, her brown eyes glistening. 'And these look *new*.' Mare strips away the straggly green grass. 'At first I thought maybe I should leave them here . . . the owner would come looking. But then I saw this.'

She points to the brand name on the snorkel. *Mares.*

'My name's right on it!' she says, laughing. 'It's obviously a gift for me!'

I don't say anything.

Mariel blows into the snorkel to clear out the airway, then wipes out the eye sockets on the goggles and adjusts them over her face. 'See ya, Willa!'

Seconds later, hip level in the water, Mariel leans face forward and she's off.

'Bye,' I shout. 'Be careful.'

That girl is so free, she amazes me. No worries about where the snorkel came from, or germs, or how she doesn't have flippers or anything. Mariel Sanchez gets an idea and swims with it.

When I first met Mare earlier this year, I didn't like her at all. She wanted my part in the play. She was after my boyfriend's heart. It seemed she was ruining my life.

I was wrong. We're getting closer now. We both love books and the beach.

I walk faster, thirstier. When I reach my bag, I fling it over my shoulder and slip on my comfy Swiss-cheese sandals, smiling at the sunflower buttons I stuck in yesterday. All my friends are wearing these shoes, decorated differently to make them unique.

As I trudge up the old grey wind-weathered

steps that lead up from the beach, everyone else is coming down. It's a perfect beach day, but I'm on lunch duty. We run the Bramblebriar Inn in town and this is our busiest season. That's the thing about a family business; the whole family helps. And we're a small family, just me, Mom and my new stepfather, Sam, whom I just started calling 'Dad'.

At the top of the steps, my best friend, Tina Belle, and my barely tolerable friend, Ruby Sivler, are getting out of the Sivlers' car. Ruby's mother toots as she zooms off, their fluffy dog, Pookie, in the passenger's seat with goggles on like the Red Baron.

Tina and Ruby are wearing bikini tops with matching orange-and-pink flowered sarongs wrapped low on their hips. They look like models on a photo shoot, like sophomores in college, not the sophomores in high school we'll be this fall. Tina flings back her long blonde hair and adjusts her silver hoop earrings. Ruby flings back her long red hair, diamond belly-ring sparkling in the sun. Tina says something and they squeal, hug-jumping like a jack-in-the-box. Two boys watch, mesmerized. The one in the Red Sox cap holds out his cellphone and shouts. Tina and Ruby wave like mermaids, hamming it up for the camera.

When Tina sees me, she looks awkward. 'Willa . . . hi. Where you going?'

'Home. I have to work.'

Ruby's lip snivels at the sound of that horrible 'w' word. 'Work' is not something a Sivler girl does. You pay people to do that sort of thing.

'You can't go, Willa,' Tina says, clutching my arm.

I feel a little less jealous now.

Ruby lowers her designer sunglasses and squints like, 'Willa, move; you're clouding my view.'

'Don't you remember?' Tina says. 'Today's the day. The last Saturday in June. *They're coming at ten!*'

'Who's coming at ten?'

Tina and Ruby look at each other, shaking their heads in disbelief. They lean towards me and whisper-shout, '*The lifeguards!*'

'Oh, right.' How could I forget?

Today's the day the college-student lifeguards

officially ascend their thrones. One bronzed, buff and beautiful prince of a boy will rule from each tall grey chair. Most beaches have boy and *girl* lifeguards, of course, but at Sandy Beach it's all boys. The lady who hires the lifeguards has three sons and they get jobs for their friends. It's a monopoly or a dynasty or some 'ee' or other. All I know is that someone is handling auditions, because I've never seen a goober yet. Every single one is hot. Tina and I used to climb the dunes with our binoculars to spy, wondering what their names were, dreaming of the day we'd be old enough to date them. We're still not old enough.

Besides, I already have a boyfriend my own age. I touch the silver heart locket around my neck. Joseph Francis Kennelly, 'JFK', gave it to me. We have a date later.

Ruby stares at the locket. 'Oh, that's right, Willa, we forgot. You're married. We understand, don't we, Tina? We won't tempt you. Will we?'

We. We. Each 'we' stings like a jellyfish. I hate you Ruby Sivler. Tina and I are the 'we'. You're the annoying third. Or at least that's how it's always been.

Ruby grabs Tina's arm and pulls. 'Come on, Teen, let's get a good spot.'

Teen?

Tina looks at me. Her eyes are sad. I can tell she's torn. I'm torn too. *BFF: Best friends forever.* How many times have we written that? Ever since I moved here to Cape Cod, we've been as tight as twins. But before I came, Tina and Ruby were best friends. They have a lot in common. Lately, it seems even more so.

'Call you later, Willa,' Tina says.

'Yeah, call me,' I say.

Biking home, the tears come. I don't want to lose my best friend. Why do I have to go to work? Why can't I just enjoy my summer like everybody else?

At the stone fence in front of our inn, I see some paper taped on the Bramble Board. We post happy quotes and town events here. On the paper is a crudely drawn bird in a red circle with a diagonal slash line through it: 'We serve plovers piping hot with fries'.

That's awful. I yank the paper off and look around. *Who would do such a thing?*

I bound up the stairs, past two guests playing checkers in the lobby, and into the kitchen for a water bottle. I chug it down and toss it in the recycling bin. *Ahhh.*

'Willa!' My stepfather, Sam, shouts, coming in from the garden.

Good, I want to show him this paper. But then I see his face. Usually a Buddha-like pillar of peaceful, Sam looks as manic as a monkey. He drops a wicker basket of green beans on the counter, spilling them everywhere. He wipes sweat from his forehead, leaving a dirty rainbow. 'Willa, I need your help.'

'Sure, Dad, anything.' My heart is pounding. I've never seen Sam so wired.

'Aunt Ruthie's coming. And she wants to get married. Here. Next week. Your mother says that's crazy, "It just can't be done," and so I'm begging you. Can you do it? Can you possibly plan a wedding in a week?'

I burst out laughing, relieved. Then Sam does too.

'Sure,' I say, 'no problem. They don't call me the wedding planner's daughter for nothing. But I have one very, very crucial question.'

'Of course, Willa, what?'

'Who the heck is Aunt Ruthie?'

2

'Greenzilla'

What is a weed?
A plant whose virtues have not yet been
discovered.

– Emerson

Ruthie is Sam's big sister. He hasn't seen her in years. An old neighbour sent Ruthie one of the bride-magazine articles about the weddings we do at the Bramblebriar Inn, and Ruthie wrote to Sam to ask if she could get married here. She's on her way home from South America right now. Ruthie works for Planet-Partners, an organization that helps bring safe drinking water to impoverished areas around the world.

'Ruthie's skinny as a string bean,' Sam says, holding up a bean to illustrate his point, 'but she'll wallop you like a watermelon.' He pounds his fist in his palm. 'She's absolutely possessed about saving the planet. Preserving waterfalls, the wilderness, the whippoorwills and wallabies, wildflowers . . . *weeds*.'

'What's wrong with that, Dad?' I pick beans up off the floor and toss the basket into the sink, turning on the water to rinse them off. 'We care about the planet too. We recycle and compost and—'

'You don't understand,' Sam says. 'Ruthie is a fanatic. "Ruthie the Ruthless", my mother used to say. She's like some evil environmental superhero. All she needs is a green cape. My sister won't stop until she single-handedly saves the planet, never mind how many people she drives batty in the process.'

'Dad, come on,' I say, spraying water over the beans, wiping off the garden dirt. I'm trying not to laugh. 'Aren't you stretching the taffy a bit?'

'No, Willa, I'm not. I still have mental scars from high school. Ruthie would stand outside the bathroom with a stopwatch, timing me when I took a shower and if I exceeded my quota she'd bang on the door screaming, "Do you know how many gallons of water you wasted, Sam? Do you? Do you know how many people will die from thirst today, Sam, while YOU are wasting precious potable water? DO YOU KNOW HOW MANY? Do you, Sam?" My friends used to call ahead of time to make sure Ruthie wasn't home before they came over. Once, I was eating a ham sandwich with my girlfriend Becky, and Ruthie lunged at us in the kitchen, sobbing, 'How can you eat something that had eyes! *Eyes!* Two of them. Probably brown ones just like you, Becky.'

'Becky lost her lunch on the spot. Me, I lost Becky.'

I burst out laughing.

'*Willa*,' Sam says. 'This is serious. Ruthie's not human. She's a lean green menacing mean ma—'

'Sam!' I shut off the water, dry my hands off quickly on a towel. I walk over and rest my palm on Sam's shoulder, and look into his eyes. 'It's OK, Dad. Settle down. Take a deep breath.' I model breathing. 'There you go. In, out, in, out. That's right. Good.'

Sam seems to calm down a bit.

'So Aunt Ruthie's a *Greenzilla*? Piece a cake. I've watched Mom handle Bridezillas for years. I've got the Stella skills. You'll see.'

I can't wait to meet this lady. This is gonna be a blast!

'You don't understand,' Sam says. 'Your mother and Ruthie are complete opposites, north-and-south-pole opposites. They'll drive each other crazy. Your mother's a neat freak; Ruthie's a slob. Stella likes rules and order. Ruthie likes reiki and oracle readings. Just wait till you see her moon salutations.'

Oh my god this is going to be great. Wait till I tell Tina!

'But . . .' Sam takes another good deep cleansing breath. 'She is my only sister.' He's calmer now, that good old Sam-the-man reason returning. 'And she's not expecting anything big for her wedding,' he pulls a folded-up letter out of his shirt pocket and looks it over. 'It's just going to be Ruthie and her fiancé, Spruce, and a few close friends.'

'His name is Spruce?'

'I know,' Sam says, smiling, 'but who knows,

he might be a great guy. They're heading off to Washington right after the wedding for the Greenvolution March on the fourth of July. Ruthie says she'd like the wedding outdoors, nothing fancy. It just has to be strictly 'eco-friendly' with no animals injured in the process or unnecessary waste of . . .'

My mother comes in. Sam stops talking. We're both extra sensitive around her these days. Mom had a miscarriage last month, and we all feel horrible, but nobody's supposed to talk about it. I feel bad for my mother, and for Sam, and me. I was excited about having a baby sister or brother, but it's a silent subject. Sam, Nana – we've all been extra-specially considerate, but my mother deals with pain by building ice-barge barricades around herself. I try, but sometimes it's hard to be nice to ice.

'Willa, please check the vases on the tables before lunch,' she says. 'Be sure they have fresh water. And I don't want any deadheads on the dahlias.'

'Sure, Mom,' I say. I lower my voice. 'Don't worry, Sam. Give me the letter. I'll come up with a plan. Oh, and, wait, I have something to show you.'

I hand Sam the nasty paper about the piping plovers. He reads it and frowns.

'I'll look into this,' Sam says. 'This I can handle. Fair-trade barter, OK?'

'What?'

'Ruthie will explain the concept to you. She won't expect to pay a cent for the wedding. She'll offer some sort of service in exchange. Do our star readings or—'

Oh my gosh. This is going to be great.

'Fair trade of worries, OK?' I say to Sam. 'You tackle the plover pirates. I'll tackle Ruthie the Ruthless. Deal?'

'Deal.'

'Done.'

Sweet Rosie Sweets

A friend may well be reckoned the masterpiece of nature.

— **Emerson**

It's nearly three when we finish clearing the lunch trays from the sun porch. 'Everyone raved about the triple-berry shortcake,' I tell my friend Rosie, our baker and assistant head chef.

'Thank you, Willa.' Rosie says, quietly. She steals a glance at my mother, who is sitting at the table doing paperwork. 'But you can't really miss with fresh berries in season.'

'Don't be modest, Rosie,' I say, stacking plates in the dishwasher. 'You are *soooo* talented. That shortcake was sublime.'

I look quickly at my mother. As expected, she

rolls her eyes about 'sublime'. What's the use of cool words if you can't show them off now and then?

'And what was that spice in the shortcake, Rosie? It was familiar, but I couldn't say for sure. Everybody was just buzzing about dessert. That big family-reunion group from New Jersey, the Moscatellos, asked if it could be on the menu again tonight, and the Red Hat ladies from Rhode Island wondered if you'd please share the recipe for the cookbook they're writing.' We love it when a Red Hat group comes to visit us at the inn. All the ladies wear purple outfits and red hats. You have to be at least fifty years old to join, but let me tell you, these ladies look great and, wow, do they have *fun*!

'They're writing a cookbook?' Rosie says.

'Yes,' I say, 'It's called Red Hot Hats in the Kitchen.'

My mother clears her throat and looks at the clock. I know Stella's thinking let's hurry up, it's getting late and there's lots to do.

'You know what, Rosie?' I say. 'I think you should write a cookbook about desserts. Nobody does sweets like you. And my grandmother knows publishers Sales people from publishing companies call on her at Sweet Bramble Books. You could do a whole series. A pie book, a cake book, a cookie book. And you should have your own TV show too. You could call it Rosie's Sweets . . . or Sweet Rosie Sweets . . . or Rosie, Sweet and Simple.'

My mother sighs loudly.

Rosie laughs and shakes her head. 'Willa, enough.'

'That's right, Willa, enough,' my mother says. 'You're embarrassing Rosie.'

Even though the *Cape Cod Times* wedding supplement called the Bramblebriar Inn signature wedding cake Rosie created the 'crème de la crème wedding cake to copy this season', and our good family friend, Chickles Blazer, of the Blazer Buick fortune – we hosted her daughter Suzanna Jubilee's wedding here last month – says it's the best cake she's ever tasted (and, trust me, Mama Blazer has sampled her fair share of frosting) Rosie continues to be absolutely mouse-modest about her confectionery genius.

I cut myself a second helping of shortcake. *Mmmmm, yum.* Rosie plops another dollop of whipped cream on top. 'Nutmeg,' she whispers, and winks at me.

My mother stands up with some envelopes in her hand. 'Would you drop these off at the post office on your way home, Rosie?'

'Sure thing, Stella.'

I walk outside with Rosie. I ask her if she'll make a cake for Ruthie Gracemore's wedding next Saturday night and help me plan the dinner too. She says, 'No problem, and tell Stella to put me on the schedule that night. I'll oversee the kitchen.'

'But you're working the Caldor wedding all Saturday afternoon,' I say. 'You'll be exhausted.'

'Don't worry about me, Willa. I'm a big girl. I want things to be just right for Sam's sister's wedding. Your father is such a good man. I'd do anything to help him out, and *you*. Besides, I need the money.'

When I go back inside the kitchen, Stella is waiting for me with her arms folded across her chest. 'Willa, I would appreciate it if you didn't actively try to get our employees to leave us.

It's hard enough finding good help on the Cape without—'

'Is that how you think of Rosie, Mom? As "help"? Rosie is our friend.'

My mother huffs. 'There's nothing derogatory about the term "help", Willa. We have several workers we count on. Rosie, Daryl, Makita . . . we couldn't run this place without them . . . and Betty and Mae-Alice, the housekeeping staff . . . the laundry girls.'

'*The laundry girls?*'

'You know who I mean, the girls who wash the linens. We've got thirty rooms in the inn, plus all the cottages, six clean bath towels in each room every day, and then there's the sheets, pillowcases, tablecloths and napkins—'

'Don't the laundry girls have names?'

'Oh, Willa, please, they're part-timers. Mae-Alice hires them. I pay their cheques. Simple as that. This is a business.'

'But this is our home too. Rosie is like a sister to me. Maybe we won't be so close to everyone, but we should at least know the names of the people who work here.'

'Fine,' my mother says, standing up abruptly.

When Stella is done, she's done. There's never a question who's boss. She didn't earn her MBA in a beauty pageant, although she could win any beauty contest she entered. My mother is stunning. Sleek black hair, jade-green eyes, peach-perfect skin. And she knows how to run a business. My mother ran one of New England's most successful wedding-planning businesses. Now she runs one of the hottest inns on Cape Cod and we host weddings here.

When I was younger, she wouldn't let me anywhere near her wedding-planning studio. She was worried I would grow up with my head in the clouds waiting for prince charming instead of working hard in school. But she finally realized she doesn't have to worry about me. I've got my sights set straight on college. And so, just this past year, she let me assist her with the weddings. We did two weddings together for good friends last month. Suzanna Blazer – I mentioned her mother before – and our town minister, Sulamina Mum. And I was maid of honour at both! It was a magical month.

My mother huffs and crosses her arms again. 'Why don't you come to the next staff meeting, Willa, and we'll have everybody introduce themselves.'

'Fine, mother. I will.' I huff back and cross my arms. 'Oh, and Sam said he talked to you about his sister Ruthie wanting to get married here next Saturday. I know we have the Caldor-Hollister wedding at eleven, with the reception on the lawn at one, but if I plan Ruthie and Spruce's wedding for that night, say around six o'clock out in the labyrinth, would that be OK?'

'His name is *Spruce*?' My mother rolls her eyes, 'Oh pa-lease. What is he, a pine tree? I heard Ruthie's a tree-hugger, but . . .'

'I know, Mom, but, *come on,* it's Sam's only sister and we've never even met her.'

Mom sighs. 'I told Sam that planning a wedding in a week was out of the question and that we have a booking earlier that day and that Katie Caldor has my complete attention all—'

'Mom, listen. What if I take care of everything, every detail about Aunt Ruthie's wedding, so you won't even have to think about it. Would that be OK?'

We hear loud laughter outside and turn towards the window. My mother smiles as she sees two of the Red Hats riding up and down on the new see-saw Sam put in last month. Sam set up swings and a sand-box too. He said it was for younger guests at the inn, but I think he had the baby in mind. Poor Sam. I hope maybe they'll try again.

'Come on, Mom. Family is important. She is Sam's only sister after all.'

'OK, Willa, enough with the guilt.' Mom shakes her head and frowns. Then her eyes meet mine and I smile. Her face brightens and she smiles too. 'As always, Willa, your heart is in the right place. And I appreciate your enthusiasm. And it is summer vacation and you did do such a lovely job helping me plan the weddings last month. I'd say you've passed your apprenticeship with flying colours.'

'Thanks, Mom.'

My mother looks out through the open door. A breeze ruffles her hair. She smiles as she watches a Red Hat climb up the slide. 'OK, Willa. Go ahead.

You have my blessing. We'll consider this your solo-flight wedding planning debut.'

Wahoo! 'Thanks, Mom!' I hug her.

My first wedding. Wahoo!

Just wait until Tina hears.

4

Wild Rhymes

'Tis the good reader that makes the good book;
in every book he finds passages which seem
    confidences or asides
hidden from all else and unmistakably meant for
    his ear.

– Emerson

I head up to my room, exhausted. Good time for
a catnap, not that we have cats, just the barn cats
that roam the fields. Real pets would be way too
messy for my mother. Stella likes things squeaky
clean. Paw prints on a Persian carpet or cat hairs
on a white wing chair would drive her mad. When
I need a pet fix, I go to Nana's and hang out with
her scrappy dog, Scamp, and his sister, Muffles, a

big old fluffy grey cat who loves the sunny window ledge at Sweet Bramble Books.

Tired from my walk and work, I hit the pillow.

An hour later, I wake up. I reach for my book, *Green Angel*, by Alice Hoffman. It's a short book and I only have a few pages left. I'm trying to read a book a day for the entire month of June. I asked Mrs Saperstone, my librarian friend, to suggest some short but powerful books – I'm calling them 'skinny-punch' books – then I asked Nana to order them for me in paperback. I like having my own copies of books so that I can read them with a pen in my hand, marking things that move me. I write the date on the inside front cover when I finish reading it, so that when I look back some day, I can see what I was thinking about and feeling all that time. Sam taught me that trick. Sam is an English teacher by profession. Now he helps run the inn, he's our main chef instead.

Yesterday I read *Bronx Masquerade* by Nikki Grimes. It's about a bunch of kids who sort out big issues in their lives by writing poetry, which they read aloud at school every Friday. I can't wait to tell JFK about it. He likes writing rhymes.

I open the drawer of my night table and take out my trusty bag of saltwater taffy, unwrap a lemon-lime, 'lemmego-lime' Nana calls it, and pop it in. Mmmm, yum.

I mark many pages of *Green Angel*, underlining beautiful images, writing 'nice', 'yes' and 'love that' in the margins. In the story, fifteen-year-old 'Green' is learning to heal and find hope after losing her family in a disaster. In the end, she decides she will tell their stories:

Every white page looked like a garden, in which anything might grow.
I sat down at the table with the pen and ink. I spread out the clean, white pages.
Then and there, I began to tell their story.

So lovely, so hopeful. This is definitely going on my 'Willa's Pix' list of recommended books.

I look at the clock. Almost time to get ready for my date with JFK. I pick up the book on Emerson that Sam bought for me. Ralph Waldo Emerson was a famous nineteenth-century American poet and essayist. I first discovered this book in

Sam's study upstairs, and when Sam noticed how interested I was, he ordered me my own copy so I could mark it up, making the book my own. Sam says I read like a writer.

To me reading and writing are inseparably connected. Some day I want to write books. My wonderful Gramp Tweed, whom I loved so much, told me he thought I'd be a writer. Gramp said the best way to prepare for that was to read all the best books I could. That was very good advice.

Emerson kept a journal just like I do. On 27 June 1839, he wrote:

I wish to write such rhymes as shall not suggest a restraint,
but contrariwise the wildest freedom.

The wildest freedom, nice. I like that. I wonder if JFK has written any more rhymes? He writes rap lyrics, good ones, about important things. JFK says rap is like poetry, but it's music. I look at the clock. He'll be here soon. He wouldn't tell me where we were going, but he's awfully excited about it. He said he wanted to surprise me.

I shower and get dressed, pull on a pink T-shirt and my favourite denim shorts. I put on some make-up, towel-dry my hair, scrunching up curls on one side, combing straight the other, my signature hairstyle: 'the Willa'. Ruby Sivler actually invented it for me. At least there's that one nice thing between us. I think about Tina and Ruby hanging out together, checking out the lifeguards at the beach, and then I push that thought from my mind.

I pick up my locket, open the heart, smile at the faces, JFK on one side, me on the other, snap the heart shut and clasp the chain around my neck.

JFK comes to the kitchen door like I asked. That way we won't have to make chit-chat with the guests on the front porch. The Red Hats got one look at my guy last night and nearly locked him up in the library so they could talk to him, they were all so absolutely smitten.

JFK was a good sport. He's always such a good sport.

But today I'm being selfish. I want my boyfriend all to myself.

JFK is wearing long tan shorts and a yellow

polo shirt. His brown hair is streaked lighter from the summer sun, nearly collar-length and wavy.

'Ready?' He smiles with those sea-blue eyes I could sail to Singapore in.

'Ready,' I say.

Chef Sam looks over at us from the stove. 'Have a good time,' he says.

'Thanks, Mr Gracemore,' JFK says.

'Bye, Dad. See ya later.'

'Where are we going anyway,' I ask JFK. 'You've had me wondering all day.'

'You'll see,' he says, smiling. 'You won't be disappointed. But bring a jacket. It could get chilly.'

We take our bikes. It's still gorgeous out. I love these long summer days.

Passing through town I see Nana's store, Sweet Bramble Books, a combination bookstore and candy shop, is bustlingly busy. We love the tourists. In July and August Bramble balloons to three times its normal size with summer visitors. Small stores like Nana's depend on that business.

Biking side by side, I tell JFK about Emerson,

the part about rhymes and freedom. 'How's your writing coming?' I ask.

'It was flowing today,' he says. 'I was mowing the lawn, mindless, and then all of a sudden, over the roar, I started getting more lines about the war. Hey, that rhymes.' He smiles. 'Flags can't hide the body bags. Had enough talk. Time to walk. People dying. Stop the lying. Don't see *your* kids on the line fighting. Made in America.'

'Whoa,' I say. 'Powerful.'

'What about you?' he says. 'Writing any more letters to stir up trouble?'

He means the letter I wrote to the *Cape Cod Times* about the lack of affordable housing on Cape Cod – seeing Mariel's living conditions made me look into the issue. My letter inspired a recently retired couple, the Barretts from New Seabury, to set up a fund to help build homes for low-income families.

'No, I've just been writing my journal.'

JFK leads us towards Sandy Beach, way down at the far end. When we come up over the hill, we leave our bikes by the rocks, stepping around the cinnamon-sweet smelling rugosa, beach roses. JFK takes my hand. 'Guessed the surprise yet?'

'No,' I say. 'I haven't got a clue.'

He squeezes my hand. 'Wait till you see.'

At the top of the steps he stops and points. 'There she is, by the jetty.' His face is shining like a kid at the Swedish-fish bin in Nana's store. 'Isn't she beautiful?'

I look down.

No, it can't be.

It is.

A boat.

It has a red and white striped sail with a black fish on top.

I gulp. Oh no. I can't.

No way can I go sailing.

5

Sailing Lessons

Every sweet hath its sour . . .

– Emerson

'What's a matter, Willa?' JFK is staring at me. 'You look scared.'

I look at him. He looks disappointed.

'No, I'm fine,' I say. 'Just surprised, that's all.' Images of the boat tipping, me sinking, are filling my mind. 'Wow, this is great. Awesome.'

'Come on,' JFK says, starting down the steps, all excited again

I follow, feeling seasick inside. *Just tell him, Willa, he'll understand. No, you'll spoil it for him. Look how happy he is!*

'I've been saving for a boat,' JFK says, 'but I was still a couple of hundred dollars short. Then my parents pulled this out of the hat. They saw my report card and went squirrelly. Straight As, but don't tell anybody. I don't want to spoil my image.' He smiles with that dimple to die for.

Don't think about dying. Nothing will bite you. You will not drown.

'And, get this,' JFK says. 'They said if I pull straight As again next year, they'll buy me a used car for my sixteenth birthday. Sweet, huh?'

'Nice bribe,' I say.

'You're not kidding,' JFK says. 'That's what thinking about college will do to otherwise sane and normal penny-pinching parents. I watched the process with my big sister, Kerry. They would have done anything to help her get into Skidmore. She had her heart set on that school. Me, I've been planning on Boston College since I was in fourth grade. My teacher, Miss Spooner, went there. I had a crush on her. Every boy in the school did. Besides, my Dad went to BC and my grandfather too, but these days it's almost impossible to get in. You've got to have great grades, ace the SATs, be a star athlete, a musical prodigy and be saving the world somehow.'

'Well, you're awesome at baseball, the best on the team, and you're doing great community service,' I say. In freshman year alone, our class helped save the Bramble Library and then did a children's-book drive. We gathered enough books to furnish a whole library for a school hit by the hurricane in Louisiana. My dear friend Sulamina Mum, she was our minister, and her husband, Riley, took the books with them to deliver when they moved to the South last month. I miss Mum. I wish she'd write.

'Enough about school,' JFK says, 'this is summer vacation. That's all I care about.' He hands me an orange life jacket.

I take it like it's a tarantula.

'Willa.' JFK shakes his head. 'You're acting strange. You've sailed before, right?'

'Sure,' I say, snapping on the jacket like I'm strapping into the electric chair.

Just tell him the truth, Willa, he'll understand.

'Well, don't you *like* to sail?' JFK says. 'You don't seem psyched.'

'Oh no, I love it.' *Liar.* I look away. My gaze lands on a sandcastle someone made earlier. It's three-tiered like a wedding cake, decorated with shells. There are even two little plastic figures on top.

'Great, then,' JFK says, smiling, snapping his jacket on too. 'You might want to leave those here,' he says, pointing to my sandals.

I take them off and throw them up on the sand. One lands on the cake castle, knocking off one of the figures. *Oops, sorry*.

JFK pushes the boat into the water. 'The wind is perfect right now.' He adjusts some ropes. 'Hand me the rudder, will you?'

I reach for something. It's the wrong thing.

'That's the daggerboard,' JFK says, laughing. 'You've done this before, right?'

'Yes, I told you. What do you think, I'm lying?' *Now I definitely can't back out*.

JFK is staring at me. 'Are you sure you're OK with this?'

The wind lifts my air. 'Yes, fine, let's go.' *Be brave, Willa, be brave*.

'You get in first and I'll push us out,' JFK says.

The boat rocks gently when I get in. It rocks more when he heaves himself in and sits beside me. His arm feels safe and strong next to mine. *Fine, this is going to be fine.*

With one hand, JFK releases the rope. The sail puffs with wind and we're off. With the other hand he moves the rudder and steers us out on to the open sea.

'When's the last time you went sailing?' JFK says.

We're already passing a buoy. I'm way out over my head. My hands are gripping the hull. 'It's been a few years.' I don't look at him.

'Well, nothing's changed,' JFK says, all happy and proud, captain of his ship. 'Wind is wind. When I say duck, duck.'

Duck, duck, silly goose Willa Havisham. What were you worrying about? See how nice this is? Safe and slow, no worries.

'Beautiful,' JFK says, smiling. 'I love this.'

He releases the line some more and the sail billows full and now we are moving, moving fast. 'Nice,' he shouts, laughing. 'Isn't this great?'

'Yeah,' I manage to say. Then I think about the jellyfish that summer when I was ten. I had just gotten my Red Cross swimming certificate, passed with flying colours, and Nana allowed me to swim out to the buoy line. I was so happy, free as a fish, when a stinging pain like a needle shot into my arm. It stunned me and I panicked. I started flailing around in the water, trying to see what had bitten me. Was it a shark? A whole school of them? What if they were surrounding me? I screamed for help, *HELP!*, waving frantically towards Nana on the shore. She waved back. She thought I was waving! I was too far out for her to hear me over the sound of the waves and all the people on the beach. It was June, before the lifeguards ascended their thrones. I waved and waved and Nana waved back. No, I'm not waving, I'm dying. *Help!* Oh my God, I thought, what if I die out here? And then I thought of my birth father, Billy Havisham, who actually did die at sea when his hot-air balloon crashed into the Atlantic Ocean the day after he and Mom married. His body was never found . . .

'Willa! Willa! What's wrong with you!' JFK is shouting at me.

'I . . . I . . . nothing.' I manage a smile, gripping the hull so tightly my hands are numb.

Faster and faster. Wind zipping through my air. Sea spray on my face.

'Whoo-hoo!' JFK shouts, his face beaming bright.

We're speeding now. It's OK. *Be brave, Willa, be brave.*

Our side of the boat rises high in the air, then higher, higher, higher, as the sail strains full with wind.

JFK's laughing. 'Yes! Ha-ha! This is it!'

Then the wind changes and the sail wobbles and whooshes. 'Duck!' JFK shouts.

I freeze.

'Duck! Willa, now, watch out!'

JFK pushes me down hard, just before the sail swings over my head.

'Jeez, Willa,' JFK says, laughing. He reaches out a hand to help me back up. 'That's a good way to get beheaded.'

'*Take me back,*' I scream. '*Now!*'

'Willa, what's wrong?' He looks shocked. 'It's OK. I know what I'm doing.'

'Take me back. I mean it.' My body is shaking scared. 'Now, Joseph, please.'

As we head back to the beach, I tell him about the jellyfish and how I haven't swim over my head in the ocean since, and how I still have nightmares about my birth father, swimming terrified out in the raging sea, engulfed by house-sized waves.

'But I've seen you swimming,' JFK says. 'You're like a fish at Dean's Pond.'

'That's a lake,' I explain. 'It's ocean swimming I'm scared of. I'm OK if I can stand. It's when I get over my head that I panic.'

'We weren't going to tip,' JFK says. 'I've been sailing since I was seven. I know what I'm doing. And besides, why didn't you just tell me.' There's an edge of anger in his voice.

I'm expecting him to be sympathetic. I just poured out my heart to him.

'Why did you lie to me, Willa,' he says, standing up. 'Don't you trust me?'

'I'm sorry.'

'I said, don't you trust me?'

'Joseph, yes, of course I do.'

'Well, you have a weird way of showing it. Come on, hop out.'

I step out into the shallow water, walk up on to the beach.

JFK pulls the boat up on shore. He wraps a wire around the rudder and centreboard and locks them, stuffs the life jackets underneath the hull.

'Come on,' he says. 'I'll take you home.'

'Joseph, please. Don't be mad.'

'It's all right,' he says.

'We still have time,' I say. 'Why don't we go for a walk or something?'

'No, I'm going home for dinner. Coach wants us over to the field early. We're working concessions for the Cape league game tonight.'

'Why don't I meet you there,' I say.

JFK still looks mad. 'No. I mean, you can do what you want, but I won't be able to hang out. Like I said, I'll be doing concessions.'

'OK, sure,' I say.

When we bike up to the inn, I say, 'Call me.'

'Yeah, sure, Willa. See ya later.'

After dinner I pull out my journal. I always feel better when I write, especially if I'm down. I pour all my doubts and fears and confusing feelings out on to the page and then slowly I start to feel better. *Learn a lesson from this, Willa. You've got to trust the people you love.*

I stare at that word 'love' for a long time. What does that even mean?

Someone's knocking on my door.

'Willa,' Daryl says. Daryl is front-desk manager tonight. 'You have a friend downstairs.'

'Thanks, Daryl.' *Tina, yes.* I slip my journal into the hiding spot between the mattress and box spring. Tina will know exactly how to handle my fiasco with JFK.

Tina Belle understands the mysteries of the male mind.

6

No Mutts About It

Two may talk and one may hear,
but three cannot take part in a conversation
of the most sincere and searching sort.

— **Emerson**

As soon as we're in up my room, Tina closes the door and says, 'Guess what? Big news. Ruby's family just bought the house next door to you, where you and Stella used to live before she married Sam.'

'What? Why? The Sivlers already have a huge house.'

I go to my window and look across the lawn to the brick house that was my first home in Bramble. It's been vacant since Mom and I moved in here with Sam.

'The Sivlers aren't going to live there,' Tina says, laughing.

'So they're going to rent it out?'

'Nope,' Tina says, plopping down on my bed, smiling like a toddler with a secret. 'Keep guessing. This is fun. See if you can figure out what they're opening there.'

'So it's a business? I don't think they can do that. This is a residential area.'

'Actually,' Tina says in a serious tone, all proud that she has inside information, 'I heard Ruby's parents talking about that very thing. Mr Sivler said the building is "zoned commercial". Your mother ran Weddings by Havisham on the first floor. That was a business. And before you moved here, it was Bramble Funeral Home.'

'Oh, right,' I say. 'I remember the estate agent telling us about the funeral home when we took the lease. I was a little spooked at first, but then I forgot about it. Wait . . . they're not opening a *funeral home* are they?'

Tina giggles. 'Yeah, right,' she says, enjoying this. 'No. Come on, Willa, seven questions. You win, I buy you a sundae at Bloomin' Jean's. I win, you buy me some water. I'm on a diet. Deal?'

'Deal.'

'Done.'

'OK,' I say. 'Is it a restaurant?'

'No.' Tina shakes her head. 'That's one.'

'A clothing store?'

'No. That's two.'

'I can count, Tina. Is it a jewellery store?'

'No. That's three.'

'Is there another business like it already in Bramble?'

'Good question, Willa. No. That's four.'

Hmmm. 'Is it a product place or a service place?'

'Excellent question,' Tina says. 'Well, I'm sure they'll have products for sale, but the main thing is service. And by the way, that's five.'

'A service, *hmmmm*, I'm thinking a spa, but there's already the Sea Spa in town and you said there wasn't anything like it in Bramble. Is it a service I would use?'

Tina giggles. 'No, definitely not. That's six. Give up?'

'No. I get one more question.' I think about

the Sivlers. How loud and flashy and tacky they are. Mrs Sivler wearing low-cut tops, slinky skirts and spiked heels at Bramble Academy events and on a Sunday at Bramble United Community, BUC, rhymes with luck, our non-denominational community church.

There's a knock on the door. 'Yes?' I say.

Sam pops his head in. 'Oh, hi, Tina.'

'Hi, Mr Gracemore. I like the new flower boxes out front.'

'Thank you, Tina,' he says, smiling. 'Willa, there's someone downstairs for you.'

'Thanks, Dad.'

He closes the door.

'*Dad?*' Tina says. 'Since when are you calling Sam Dad?'

'Since Father's Day.'

'It's probably Joseph downstairs,' Tina says, fixing her hair in the mirror.

'No, Sam would have said. And besides, Joseph's mad at me.' I quickly tell her the sailing story.

'I don't blame you, Willa,' Tina says, ever the best friend taking my side. 'You wouldn't catch me out on one of those little Sunfishes either.

They look like baby bathtub boats for gosh sakes. A real boat gets too close and you're in with the fish. Yachts are much more civilized. You've been out on our *Salty Princess*. Now that's a boat. You can sprawl out and sunbathe on the deck, have a formal dinner down below, shower, sleep—'

'Come on, Tina,' I say. 'Let's see who's down-stairs.' Tina follows me.

Mariel Sanchez is in the games room, playing cards with the Red Hat ladies. The women are decked out in purple outfits with red cowboy hats, all set to head out to the Garth Brooks concert at the Melody Tent.

Mariel waves and smiles when she sees us.

'Hi, Mare,' I say.

'Willa . . . Tina . . . hi.' Mare stands up from card table. 'Gotta go, ladies, goodbye. Don't do anything I wouldn't do.' The Red Hats laugh.

Mare walks towards me and Tina, smiling. 'I was dropping off books at the library. Thought you might want to catch the baseball game or get an ice cream.'

'Actually, that's where we were heading,' I say.

Mare looks at Tina. 'I saw you and Ruby at the beach today.'

'Yeah, I saw you too,' Tina says. She looks down at Mariel's feet.

Mariel is wearing sneakers, not Swiss-cheese sandals like us.

'Are you a member of the BBA?' Tina asks Mariel.

That's short for Bramble Beach Association. Tina knows Mariel isn't.

'No,' Mare says, 'why?'

'Because Sandy Beach is privately owned and—'

'Hey, girls,' I say, interrupting. 'Baseball or ice cream?' I move into the centre between them as we walk into town. I'm hoping they say baseball so I can see JFK.

'Let's hit Norma's first, then head over to the field,' Tina says, flipping her hair back, decision done. 'Ruby's father is sponsoring the game tonight.'

We walk towards the ice-cream parlour in silence.

'So, Tina,' I say, 'you didn't tell me. How do the lifeguards look this year?'

'Same as always,' Tina answers.

Several more seconds of silence. 'Mariel,' I say, 'Tina was telling me about a new business moving in next door to our inn.'

'Really,' Mare says, leaning around me to look at Tina. 'That's interesting, what?'

Tina shrugs her shoulders.

'Come on, Tina,' I say. 'Give it up. Dish the news.'

Tina gives me an annoyed look. 'It's nothing important.'

'Well then, what is it?' Mariel says.

Tina just keeps walking.

'Come on, Tina,' I say jokingly. 'Don't make me beg like a dog.'

'It's a pet spa,' Tina blurts out. 'They're opening a pet spa. No big deal.'

I stop walking. Mare does too. Tina stops, then turns back to look at us.

'What do you mean . . . a *pet spa*?' Mariel asks.

Tina leans in dramatically towards Mariel, eyes squinting like Mare is from Mars. 'You *do know* what a spa is, right?'

Uh-oh. I intervene. 'So they're opening a place to take dogs to get groomed.'

Tina huffs disgustedly. 'You can do *that* at the mall, Willa. No Mutts About It will be a four-star luxury resort for our four-legged friends. Beauty treatments, massages, overnight lodging in private suites, gourmet room-service dining—'

'For *dogs*?' Mariel says, appalled.

I picture the cramped room where Mariel's entire family is living in that ugly old run-down motel on the edge of town, all they can afford even though their father works full-time . . . warming up meals in a microwave, no kitchen . . .

'Yes,' Tina says, hands on her hips. 'Do you have a problem with that?'

'Yes,' Mariel says in a quiet voice, 'I do.'

'You know what, Willa,' Tina says. 'I'm not into ice cream any more. I'll catch up with you guys at the game.'

'Tina, wait.' She doesn't stop.

'I'm sorry, Willa,' Mariel says quietly. 'Go with your friend.'

'No,' I say. 'That's all right. I have a problem with the pet spa too.'

When Mariel and I get to the field, they are just finishing the national anthem, and then the announcer says that this evening's game is courtesy of The Sivler Group, the holding company for Sivler Realty and Construction and several other Bramble businesses, including the soon to be opened No Mutts About It. 'And everyone please join me now in a big Bramble welcome for Miss Ruby Sivler, who will be throwing out the first ball tonight.'

Mariel and I watch as Ruby swaggers out on to the green, boobs bopping in a tight red tank top, hips swaying in a short skirt. She smiles, flashing her newly whitened teeth. There's an explosion of whistles and catcalls. Ruby waves up to the bleachers, blowing kisses. I look at Mariel and we roll our eyes.

Ruby holds up the ball, arches her arm back, up and over, and lets it go. The crowd applauds and the announcer shouts, 'Play ball!'

'Where do you want to sit?' Mariel says.

I see Tina right above the dugouts, sitting with Mrs Sivler and Ruby's older sister, home for the summer from college. No mutts about it, my butt. I have no interest in talking to that family. 'Wherever,' I say, 'it doesn't matter.'

'I love baseball,' Mariel says as we find seats several rows up.

'Well, you've moved to the right place then,' I say. 'The Cape Cod Baseball League is famous. Some of the best players in the country start out here.'

At the end of the third inning, Mariel goes to the restroom and I go to the concession stand to look for JFK. There's a long queue. When I get to him, he acts nice enough, but I can tell he's still mad. He hands me the soda and takes my money.

'Joseph, hi!' Mare comes up behind me.

'Hey, Mare,' JFK says, smiling, all happy to see her.

'I didn't know you worked here,' Mare says.

'I don't,' JFK says. 'Our team is just helping out tonight.'

'I wanted to tell you,' Mariel says. 'I got that job at Shop 'n Save you were telling me about. I won't be fifteen until the end of August, but after your mother called the manager, they said I could start next week. Tell your mom I said thanks, OK?'

'Sure, Mare,' JFK says. 'But you should stop by and tell her yourself. She always likes to see you.'

Jealousy pops up, but I push it back down. *JFK and Mare are just friends, that's all. Remember, Willa? You've been through this already. Just friends.*

'Oh, and, Joe,' Mariel says, 'did you decide about the audition for—'

What audition?

'Hey, hey, hey,' a guy behind us shouts. 'Hurry up. I need a hot dog. If you want to sit around chatting, go to a soccer game. This is *baseball*.'

After the game I try to find JFK, but by the time I make my way down the bleachers and through the crowd to the concessions stand, he's gone.

Later I call his cellphone, but he doesn't answer. I check, but he's not online.

7

Beauty and the Bites

Nature and books belong to the eyes that see them.

– Emerson

The next morning I wake up in a slump. First I mess things up with JFK, then I push Tina even further away, and what if Mariel and JFK really start liking each other? I know Mare's my friend, but she's gorgeous, I don't want her over at my boyfriend's house, even if it is just to visit his mother.

It's only four a.m. Sunday. BUC is at eleven. I wonder who the new minister is? Whoever it is won't ever replace Sulamina Mum. Mum was my first friend in Bramble, almost like another mother to me. I miss her, but I couldn't be happier that she and Riley finally got together. They were high-school sweethearts, separated by the war, and time, and geography, but I worked a bit of Cape Cupid matchmaking magic, and the two of them got together. All I did was nudge Mum until she wrote him a letter. Her words did all the rest. Never underestimate the power of a letter.

I flick on the light by my bed and open up today's book, *True Believer* by Virginia Euwer Wolff. I scanned the jacket in Nana's store and it looked good. I open to the first page:

'My name is LaVaughn and I am 15. When a little kid draws a picture it is all a big face and some arms stuck on. That's their life. Well, then: You get older and you are a whole mess of things, new thoughts, sorry feelings, big plans, enormous doubts, going along hoping and getting disappointed, over and over again . . .

Nice, I'm hooked already. I like when an author writes in the 'first person'. It lets me feel like I'm right inside that character, feeling all the things she's feeling.

I read for a half-hour or so, and then remember

I need a new quote for the Bramble Board. I reach for Emerson. Old Ralph's quite the quotable guy. Here's a good one:

The only true gift is a portion of yourself.

That sounds like something Sulamina Mum would say. She always had a subtle or sometimes not so subtle way of reminding us to 'get out of ourselves' and focus on others, finding ways to serve. My dad, Sam, calls that 'community rent' – like you pay rent for housing, you should pay rent to your community too – giving a portion of your time or money or talents to help others.

This past spring when I wrote a letter to the *Cape Times* about the shortage of affordable housing on the Cape, my small letter sparked something big. My 'talent' was writing the letter. English teacher Sam, 'Dad', still getting used to that name, says words can have a powerful effect. Think about the book *Charlotte's Web*, and those two little words: 'some pig'.

If Mum was here she'd say, 'Nice job with that letter, Willa, but what are you going to do next?'

She'd say something like, 'Hmmm . . . big long summer ahead. What, two whole months at least, right? The work is never done, little sister. Don't hide your light. Go ahead now and find your next way to shine.'

I look at the clock: five a.m. Maybe I'm not too late for the sunrise. I jump out of bed, pull on shorts and a shirt. Grab my journal, and a water bottle from the kitchen, toss them in the wicker basket on my bike outside, and take off quick for the beach.

It's dark and quiet, like I'm the only person awake in the world. Then a bird sings down to me from the telephone wire above and I realize I'm not alone. As I near the water, a soft mist coats my face. The sky is filmy and cotton-candy pink.

When I reach the beach, I look out at the horizon. *Yes.* I'm not too late. And *good*, no one else is here. I sit on the top step and stare out at the scene before me. Beauty, beauty, everywhere . . . The sea is calm, silver coloured, flat like a mirror. I wonder what it would be like to look into that water, see that whole other world beneath the waves. A fish tail breaks the surface, then bobs back underneath. *Ouch.* Something bit my neck. I slap it. A tiny black bug. *Ouch*, another bit my head. I scratch. Then there's a bunch of them all around my face. Oh, great. I flap my hands. It doesn't make a difference. *Ouch.* Why didn't I bring bug spray?

Down below, a little black-capped tern, one of the endangered birds, hovers in the air above the water, searching for food. It flaps crazily in the air, fighting the wind, trying to stay in place, hovering like a helicopter pilot waiting for control-tower permission to land. It spots its prey and nosedives into the water, then right back again, empty beaked. *Sorry, little tern.*

Now the sky is a palette of pinks and purples, getting brighter, almost time. *Ouch*, I slap my leg. If I can just withstand these stupid bugs. I scratch and scratch. And then, there it is. A sliver of sun, like a salmon.

Good morning, new day. Thank you.

As it rises, the sun casts a red line across the water to me, closer and closer until it reaches the shore, bearing a sheath of sparkling rubies. I close my eyes and scoop up the jewels, locking them safe in my memory.

I open my eyes and open my journal, writing fast to capture this moment.

It was worth the bug bites. That's the way life is. There is good and bad in everything. You can either focus on the annoying things you have no way of controlling, or cast your gaze upon the glory of a bright new amazing day, hours of delightful possibility, stretching out like a summer before you.

I read over what I wrote. It doesn't do the sunrise justice at all. Such powerful beauty in nature and then I try to capture it and it sounds so small.

I flip off my sandals and walk. The cool sand feels good beneath my feet. I take deep breaths, in and out, in and out. I think about JFK and Tina and the pet spa. Knowing how she feels about animals, I'm not sure how to break the news to my mother. I let all these worries wash over me and then out to sea with the waves. I can't imagine a better way to start a day. Watching the sunrise and walking the beach. I'm a 'lucky duck indeed' as Nana would say.

Out on the end of the Spit, the area where the bird people were stringing the posts yesterday, there is a new sign. A large pay-attention sign:

AREA CLOSED
Threatened Birds Nesting

Common Tern • Least Tern • Piping Plover

If birds are disturbed, parents may leave the nest, subjecting eggs and young to exposure and possible death.

Entering this area is a violation of state and federal law.

0 / 0 / 0 /
No Vehicles•No Dogs•No Entry

These rare birds and their nests and eggs are protected under Massachusetts and federal laws.

Persons may be arrested and fined for killing or harassing or in any way disturbing birds nesting in this area.

Massachusetts Audubon Society

Just there, a few feet ahead of me, a piping plover is giving two babies a flying lesson out over the waves. I stand for a moment, watching. How beautiful they are. I wonder what Sam found out about that awful flyer someone posted on the Bramble Board.

I turn and head back along the water. I slip on my sandals, walk up the steps. I think about Tina questioning Mariel about being on this beach, like she didn't have a right to be here. When I get to the top, I look out at the scene one last time.

The sky is white now, the sun a blazing yellow yolk. Like a perfectly poached Sunday-brunch egg at the Bramblebriar Inn.

When I get home I take out the silver box on the porch and grab the letters I need to change the Bramble Board. T, H, E, O, N, L, Y, T, R, U, E, G, I, F, T . . .

I stick on the letters and step back to read:

> The only true gift is a portion of yourself.
> Ralph Waldo Emerson

The Shasta daisies Sam planted around the base of the Bramble Board are smiling up at me. I pick one and lift the sunny yellow centre to my lips, thinking of JFK. I begin to pluck the petals: he loves me, he loves me not, he loves me, he loves me not . . . Why can't I just trust JFK's feelings for me? Deep down I know how much he cares for me, so why do I feel worried? I shake off these thoughts and toss the flower down before I reach the last petal.

I hurry up the stairs and head to the kitchen. A cup of tea before BUC sounds good.

8

Family Day

*I like the silent church before the service
  begins,
better than any preaching.*

– Emerson

As we're walking to BUC, I tell Sam about the
endangered birds sign I saw posted out on the
Spit.

Bramble United Community is a place where all
people are welcome no matter your background,
no matter your beliefs. We come together once
a week to 'to be grateful'. Our former minister,
Sulamina Mum, used to say the only prayer you
ever need is just two words long. Thank you.

Jew, Catholic, Baptist, Buddhist, Atheist,

Agnostic, whatever 'ist' you ist or isn't, we all share a common belief in the goodness of the human spirit, a gratitude for our lives and a sense of responsibility to the greater world community.

'I asked around town yesterday, Willa,' Sam says, 'but I couldn't find out anything about that plover flyer. Probably just somebody's strange idea of a practical joke. I don't think it's anything more than that.'

'But why did they post it on our Bramble Board?' I say.

'Because the board is Bramble's centre of "buzz",' Sam says.

'Buzz' is way too wrong for a father to be saying, but I don't roll my eyes.

'It's like they say about us in the inn guide books,' Sam says, 'People read the Bramble Board to get inspired and to find out what's cooking around town.'

'Cooking' is even cornier, but I let Sam slide.

BUC isn't very crowded. Many year-round residents holiday off-Cape in July to escape the clogged roads and crowded restaurants. Some, especially those near the shore, rent their houses out to tourists in the summer.

Up at the pulpit, in a fancy black robe with a red velvet collar, is Dr Theodore J. Deadham of Harvard Divinity School, 'Most recently of the First Unitarian Universalist Society of Boston.' When he looks our way, I smile at him. He doesn't smile back.

Dr Deadham reads his entire sermon in a loud, booming voice, without ever pausing to look at us. It's the worst service ever. That man found five ways to remind us he was from Harvard in the first five minutes, but didn't say anything I will remember. He might have the smartest brain on the planet, but he didn't move my heart at all.

I tried to be open-minded and open-hearted, really I did, Mum would have demanded nothing less, but Dr Deadham was so puffed up with his own self-importance I fully expected to him to sprout peacock feathers at any given moment. Blue, green, yellow, red.

'We should at least give him the benefit of a second chance,' Sam said quietly as we congregated in the gathering space for bagels and doughnuts.

Sam is a teacher, you have to forgive him. I think teachers are genetically wired to be kind and encouraging.

'Completely uninspiring,' was my mother's more callous critique.

'Brainiac-boring,' was Tina's two cents.

'Certainly an intelligent, well-read man,' was my good friend Mrs Saperstone's assessment, 'but unfortunately doesn't seem to have a sense of humour.'

'I will reserve judgement until I've heard him speak again,' said Dr Swaminathan, my English teacher at Bramble Academy. See what I mean about the genetic wiring? Dr Swammy, as he's known affectionately – he's such an amazing teacher – is just back from India. Sam filled in for him while he was away. It was so cool having Sam as my teacher. I was so proud. I kept looking around the classroom wanting to say, 'Do you all realize this man is my father?'

'What did you think of Dr Deadham, Willa?' Sam says as we're walking home.

'On a scale of one to ten, compared to Mum, I guess I'd give him a two.'

'Two's too generous,' Nana says. 'But, that's the last we'll be seeing of the doc, anyway.'

'What do you mean, Nana?'

'I did a quick check-in with the other members of the BUC Board of Directors and there was an overwhelming consensus. We test out ministers and vote before we formally offer a candidate the position. This is a plum job, Willa. We're a great community here in Bramble. You know that. We won't settle for anything less than the best. We broke it to Dr Dead gently. I bet he's halfway home to Beantown as we speak.' Beantown is our nickname for Boston.

'I love you, Nana.'

We stop in front of Sweet Bramble Books. Nana lives above the store.

'Can you come by later, Willa?' Nana says. 'I'm gearing up for the vote and I need your help.'

Nana's not talking politics. She's talking taffy. Saltwater taffy, that is. I'm her official 'taste-tester' for trying out new flavours each season. *Cape Cod Life* magazine does a readers' 'best of' survey. Nana's neck and neck with Ghelfi's of Mashpee for 'best sweets on the upper cape'. She wants to win best bookstore too, and if it wasn't for Eight Cousins in Falmouth, she might. No way is she going to beat them. So with the 'best of' survey, we've got all our eggs in the candy basket so to speak.

'Ghelfi's has a gorgeous new window display, just for taffy,' Nana says, all worried, 'and they've got slick new ads boasting about their fifty-two varieties of taffy, the largest selection of any candy store on the Cape. How can I compete with that?'

'Let me think about it, Nana,' I say. 'I can't come today, but I'll come first thing tomorrow, promise.'

My mother has officially claimed Sunday as 'family day'. When we get back to the inn, Mom checks to make sure everyone has shown up for work and that there are no pressing issues she has to attend to.

'Go, Stella, go,' Daryl says, putting her hands on my mother's back, and sweetly pushing her away from the front desk. 'It's your day with your family. Go enjoy.'

I'm fairly sure my mother read something in one of her trusted business magazines about the importance of scheduling a 'family activity' every weekend. Last Sunday we took the ferry out to Nantucket, the island where Mom and Sam eloped to. Such a pretty place, so romantic. I'm glad I got to see it.

I don't mind 'family day', but today all I want to do is see JFK. Make sure he's not mad at me any more. And Tina, I need to talk to Tina. And Mariel. What audition was she talking to JFK about?

'So what's the plan, ma'am?' Sam says to my mother with a smile.

'How about a bike ride on the Rail Trail?' Mom suggests.

'Sounds good,' Sam says, patting his stomach. 'I could use some exercise. Couldn't resist a second helping of the filet mignon last night. OK with you, Willa?'

'Sure,' I say, 'but just not all day. There are some things I need to do later.'

Sam and Mom look at each other and smile.

'Teenagers,' my mother whispers shaking her head.

I roll my eyes to myself. Lately I'm starting to feel like a bit of an outsider. Mom and Sam are united, a team: 'Let me talk with your father first,' or, 'Let me just run this by your mother.' We're on the same field. But they're on one team and I'm on the other.

The Cape Cod Rail Trail is a network of paved hike trials through some of the nicest nature you've ever seen. After the railroads stopped running on the Cape years ago, someone had the excellent idea to pull up the tracks and pave over them. The 'Rail Trail', starts in Dennis and weaves through forests and fields, along marshes and cranberry bogs, past harbours and ponds (that's what we call lakes), through towns and villages, past country stores and ice-cream places, all the way out to Wellfleet.

Sam puts our bikes on the rack of his car and we drive to a Rail Trail parking lot.

As we get on our bikes, I see Sam wink at my mother and my mother smile back at him. They are so in love.

'I'll race you,' Stella shouts, and we're off.

I love this family.

9

Beach Rights

Mine and yours;
Mine, not yours.
Earth endures;
Stars abide —
Shine down in the old sea.

— Emerson

When we get home hot and sweaty from biking, Mom suggests we go to the beach. I'm about to decline, when I see the look on her face. She seems so happy and relaxed. This family-time stuff is important to her and, anyway, I'm sure Tina will be at the beach stalking lifeguards, and I need to talk with her.

Mom and I head upstairs to change. Sam says he'll pack sandwiches.

When we get to the beach, we pause at the top of the steps. Out on the Spit there's a red light swirling on the harbour master's boat and a large group of people all huddled together.

'Let's see what's going on,' Mom says.

At the bottom of the steps, I spot Tina and Ruby. They are standing at the base of a lifeguard's chair, staring up at a greased Greek god of a guy. Ruby says something and the god leans down to answer. Tina smiles, nodding her head, and writes something on a clipboard like she's taking notes. I wonder what that's all about.

Mom and Sam and I walk out on the Spit.

We hear shouting as we approach the crowd. I notice someone has ripped down the ropes and stakes from the piping plover and tern nesting area.

'Look at that,' Sam says.

There is black paint smeared over the new Audubon Society warning sign.

'Who's gonna make me?' a big-bellied man with a very red face is shouting.

'It's just for a few weeks, maybe a month . . .' says a young college-age-looking woman wearing a brown shirt with the official Audubon seal on the pocket.

'This is *our* beach,' a lady shouts. It's Ruby Sivler's mother, perched on the deck of their yacht, all tanned in a shiny pink bikini. 'We already have people sneaking on to this beach who don't belong here, taking up space. Sometimes we can't even find a place to sit.'

'That's right!' someone shouts.

'But what about the birds?' a boy says.

'I don't give a flying . . .'

'But these aren't just any old birds,' the Audubon lady says. 'The least and common terns and the piping plovers are on the endangered species list.'

An adult plover is hovering in the air by the shoreline, screeching. It circles around and soars in towards us, swiping close to Mrs Sivler's bright red hair.

'Get away, get away,' Mrs Sivler screams, flapping her arms, hysterically. 'These birds are dangerous! They don't belong here!'

'They won't attack you,' the Audubon worker explains. 'It's just a mother trying to scare you away from her chicks, that's all.'

'We have a right to enjoy our beach,' Mrs Sivler says, picking up her fluffy white poodle, Pookie, and hugging him to her chest. People . . . and their pets . . . come before *birds*.'

'That's right,' a man with a sunburned face shouts. 'People count more than plovers.'

I wonder if he's the one who put the flyer on our Bramble Board? Or, wait, what if it was Mrs Sivler?

'We all have a right to this beach,' a young college-aged man says.

'Excuse me,' Ruby Sivler's father says, standing up on his boat, cocking his captain's hat to the side, speaking with great authority, 'but that's not true. Only those property owners between Sea Bluff and Windy Road, and Shore Drive and Oak Path have actual, legally deeded rights to this beach.'

'That's right!' a lady says. 'I had to tell some boy to leave the other day. He was building a fire, all set to cook a fish, his dog was running loose. I told him this was private property.'

'Good for you,' Mr Sivler says. 'We need to protect our investment from trespassers. It's high time we instituted an identification system so we know who belongs here and who doesn't.'

'Hear, hear!' some man shouts, and a few people clap.

I spot Mariel in the crowd. She steps forward, hands on her hips. 'With all due respect, sir, if anybody owns this beach, it's the Wampanoag Indians you stole it from. They were here before the pilgrims landed. Centuries before any of you.'

Yay, Mariel. You tell him. I start to walk towards her and then stop and turn at the sound of barking.

There's a huge golden-brown shaggy dog sniffing around dangerously close to one of the silver cages the Audubon workers put over the eggs and newly hatched chicks.

'Get that dog on a leash!' someone shouts.

The dog nudges the cage as if he's trying to flip it over.

The guy with the red face claps. 'That's right! Show those birds who's top dog around here.'

'Is that your dog, sir?' Sam asks the man in a calm voice.

'Not mine,' the guy says.

The dog runs over to where Sam and Mom and I are standing. It shakes its coat and water sprays on my legs. Then the dog hunches down and poops right in front of us.

'That's disgusting,' Mom says, looking around at the faces. 'Who owns this dog? Dogs aren't allowed on this beach without a leash. It's against the law.'

The dog looks at me. Our eyes lock for a second. It doesn't have a collar. Then, I know this sounds silly, but I swear the dog smiles at me, a big goofy clownish smile like that carnival booth at the Barnstable Fair, where you throw three balls into the clown's mouth to win a stuffed-animal prize.

The dog turns and runs up over the dune and is gone.

We ended up spending a family afternoon on the beach and I agreed to go to Bobby Byrne's restaurant in Mashpee Commons for dinner. I like how they have quotes from famous writers on the walls. I order a cup of clam chowder, we call it 'chowda', and the Shakespeare Chicken Sandwich. Yum.

Next I do some undercover sleuthing at Ghelfi's Candy Store. They've added on and remodelled and they're serving ice cream now. I get the vanilla frozen yogurt with Heath-bar chunks, my favourite.

I take a long time making my saltwater taffy selections, making mental notes on all their new flavours. No way can Nana compete with their variety. We'll need to think of a different angle.

Back home, I run up to my room and close the door. I take out my cellphone and call JFK. All I get is his voice, with rap music in the background, 'Hey, this is Joe; I'm not around; so leave me a message,' *beep*.

'Hi, Joseph. It's Willa. Listen, I'm sorry again about yesterday. Call me, OK?'

I check, but he's not online either. I leave a message there too.

Aunt Ruthie's wedding. I get out her letter and my planning notebook. She said she wants simple and outdoors. I think Sam's backyard labyrinth will be perfect. The daisies and dahlias and brown-eyed Susans are in full bloom, and if we do it at six we'll still have plenty of light. Ruthie's note says her friend Michael who's coming is a minister and he'll officiate the ceremony. Note: ask Sam what kind of music Ruthie likes.

Now for the menu. I head down to the kitchen and look over the cookbook shelf. I pull three vegetarian cookbooks from the shelf and start looking through the recipes. Let's see, first course. Gazpacho would be a good choice, get to show off Sam's prized vegetables . . . or a maybe a chilled blueberry soup. Salad . . . fresh garden greens and chèvre cheese. And the famous Bramblebriar bruschetta, with fresh tomatoes and basil. The main course is harder. Everything I think of has meat or fish. Tofu turkey? No. Maybe a pasta of some sort? Here's a good one: angel-hair pasta with fresh grilled red and yellow peppers, asparagus and mozzarella. Mmm, yum.

The dessert is a piece of cake, literally. Rosie's

whipping up the signature Bramblebriar Inn wedding cake with the lucky charms in the centre well. When Rosie bakes the cake, she leaves a hollow space, a 'wishing well' I call it, on the top tier of the cake, so that I can add twelve little silver charms: a book, a rose, an angel, a butterfly, an anchor, a rainbow . . . The cake was Rosie's idea, the charms were mine. It's our new old-fashioned wedding custom. Each tiny charm is wrapped in a piece of plastic with a satin ribbon attached. I put the charms in the well, and we drape the ribbons up and out over the tiers of the cake like a waterfall. At the reception, twelve pennies will be randomly placed under dinner plates around the room. Those twelve people will get to pull a good-luck charm from the cake. So far, guests seem to love this new tradition at Bramblebriar. I like listening to people assign meanings to the charms they pull.

'Oh, it's a butterfly! I bet that means . . .'

Back upstairs I turn on my night light, open up my bag of candy and *True Believer*. I am loving this book.

Hours later, I'm finished. I'm sad because I want to read on and on. There's this one scene in which the main character, LaVaughn, has gone through a really hard time holding something inside she's been afraid to tell her mother, but finally she does and her mother rises to the occasion:

Maybe it was hours she held me there, maybe only
* minutes.*
And then she fed me supper in bed,
Her good beef and mushrooms,
And she pulled up a chair to my desk and we ate there
* in my room*
With the weeping willow tree hanging over.

I close the book and put in on my Willa's Pix shelf.

The battle on the beach over the birds comes into my mind and I open up my journal to write.

Who owns a beach? Who owns the ocean? Who owns any part of the earth? Do people have any more right to any of it than plants or animals do?

Just because we're bigger, does that make us better? Dinosaurs were bigger and look what happened to them . . .'

I yawn, close my journal, and turn off the light.

I'll figure it all out tomorrow.

10

Everyone's Writing Books

Meek young men grow up in libraries,
believing it their duty to accept the views which
Cicero, which Locke, which Bacon have given,
forgetful that Cicero, Locke and Bacon were
only young men in libraries when they wrote these
books.

– Emerson

Monday morning, I'm on breakfast duty with Mom and Makita. Rosie tells me what the specials are and I write the choices on the chalkboards in the dining room and out on the sun porch:

* Cranberry nut pancakes with Vermont maple syrup
* Cheddar cheese, apple and sausage omelette with cinnamon-swirl toast

* Blueberry yogurt with honey-nut granola and berries

* * * Muffin du Jour: cherry-chocolate * * *

'*Cherry-chocolate muffins?* I better taste-test these first,' I say, pouring myself a cup of tea from the white china pot with the blue and green flowers, a gift from Nana last Christmas. Nana insists the only civilized way to drink tea is from a teapot, none of that dunking-a-bag-in-a-mug-of-microwaved-hot-water stuff.

The tea has been steeping for three minutes and is now a perfect reddish-brown. I add a little milk, no sugar, just milk, that's the way Nana and I take our tea. Gramp Tweed and I used to drink lemon tea together, no milk, when we did our Friday afternoon 'book talks' on the couch at Sweet Bramble Books. It's funny how we have different customs with the different people in our lives. Sam drinks Yogi Tea, ginger-root is his favourite. I like it too. The bags have little messages on them like fortune-cookie bits of wisdom. Sam puts the messages he likes best on the counter in the kitchen. *Hey, that gives me an idea for Nana . . .*

I bite into the cherry-chocolate muffin, still

warm from the oven, and plop down on a chair quickly before I faint from happiness. 'Oh, my gosh, Rosie! These are *amazing*.' I lick the chocolate from my fingers. The taste reminds me of the chocolate-covered cherry cordials I used to love. Until they got me into trouble with my mother and ruined the most important wedding of her career – well, that's a whole other story. Now saltwater taffy is my favourite candy. Cape Cod is famous for it.

'Really, Rosie,' I say. 'These muffins are to die for.'

'Thank you, Willa,' Rosie says. She steals a quick look at my mother, who is filling wicker baskets with muffins, covering each with a green linen napkin.

'I mean it, Rosie,' I say. 'You should write a cookbook. I'm going to see my grandmother later. Do you want me to ask her if—'

'Willa,' my mother says loudly. 'Please start around with the coffee.'

Out on the sun porch, I look out the window. There are several trucks parked in front of our old brick house, soon to be No Mutts About It. The front door is open and the shades are all up. There are workers inside painting. Two guys are on the roof fixing something. It's strange seeing our old house being turned into something else. We had some happy times there – and some not so happy ones – but it was my first home in Bramble and so it will always be special to me.

'More coffee?' I say, circulating the porch with pots of regular and decaf, cheerfully wishing our guests good morning and enquiring how their vacations are going.

The Red Hat ladies are gushing about the concert. 'Garth's a god,' Mrs Madden says, fanning her face with an autographed picture. 'Worth every penny.' The ladies are taking the ferry out to Martha's Vineyard today and then going to a programme at the Bramble Library tonight. Mrs Saperstone is doing her annual 'Bramble Beach Reads' suggested list of good summer books. The Moscatellos are heading up to Provincetown for a whale watch. 'Don't forget to climb Pilgrim Monument,' I say. 'The view from up top is beautiful. And be sure to stop at the National Seashore on the way home. It's something you absolutely don't want to miss.'

Sam is in the corner talking with new guests who checked in last night. He introduces me to Fred and Pauline Miller and their children, Kamen and Shay.

'Mr Miller was telling me about his new book,' Sam says.

'Cool,' I say. 'What's it about?'

'About reaching our fullest potential,' Mr Miller says, 'and helping other people reach theirs.'

'Sounds interesting,' I say. 'What's it called?'

Mr Miller laughs. 'My editor's still deciding, but the working title is *Be Big*.'

'*Be Big*,' I say. 'Nice. I'd like to read it.'

'Me too,' Sam says. 'Let us know when it's out, Fred. We'll definitely need a signed copy for the Inn library and one for the Bramble Library too.'

Sam and I carry trays out to the kitchen. He looks lost in thought.

'What about you, Dad? Aren't you working on a book?'

He doesn't respond.

'That first night you invited me and Mom here for dinner, when you two were first dating, you showed us your study. I remember your desk was covered with papers and there were manuscripts piled high on the floor. You said you were working on a book. But now you never talk about it.'

Sam looks at me and then away. 'It's tough to break into the book world, Willa. I'm not sure I have the talent. Maybe some day I'll get back to it.'

'Of course you have the talent,' I say. 'You should be writing. Why aren't you writing?'

'There's never time. Running the inn is a full-time job. I had no idea we'd become so popular so fast.' Sam doesn't look happy about our success.

'Wait, Dad. Are you *happy* doing this? Opening the inn was Mom's idea. I know you miss teaching and if you want to be writing, you should have time for that. I would love to read some of your—'

'That's enough, Willa.'

Sam's voice is sharp, like a slap. Wow. He never talks like that to me.

'I'm sorry, Willa,' he says. 'It's just I don't want to talk about it.' He smiles that beautiful Sam smile, his blue eyes framed with crinkles of kindness.

'OK, Dad, sure.'

Later, biking to Tina's house, all I can think of is *what is Sam's book about*?

When I get to Tina's, her mother says Tina is at Ruby's house. I try not to show how sad that makes me feel.

'Go ahead over there, Willa,' Mrs Belle says. 'I know Tina would be sorry if she missed you.'

Ruby and Tina are coming out of the Sivler's front door when I arrive. Ruby has a camera and a notebook. Tina is carrying that clipboard I saw her with on the beach. They're laughing, all happy together. *BFF*.

I turn green. Not on the outside, of course, but sick-green to my stomach inside. Whoever named jealousy that colour was right on the money. I'm guessing Shakespeare, but I'll have to look it up. Jealousy isn't pink or purple, definitely not yellow. It's green for sure. I think of Sam calling Ruthie a lean green mean-machine. Can't wait to meet her. I hope she likes the plans I've made for her wedding.

'Willa!' Tina shouts. 'Guess what? We're making a book!'

'What kind of book?' It seems everyone's writing a book but me.

'A beach book,' Ruby says in a superior voice. She adjusts something on her camera and then checks her nails.

'Well, sort of more like a yearbook,' Tina explains, 'with photos and profiles of all the cutest lifeguards on Cape Cod. Sort of like those bios on the Internet, except ours will be a real book you can hold in your hands and get autographed.'

So that's what they were doing yesterday.

'We started with the boys on Sandy Beach,' Ruby says. 'That boy, Desmond, from Dartmouth is *delicious* isn't he, Teen?'

'So hot he's on fire,' Tina says. 'That boy ought to come with a warning label.' They laugh like they've got a secret.

'Today we're heading up to Chatham,' Ruby says.

'We're doing one beach a day,' Tina says.

I'm reading a book a day. Tina's reviewing one beach a day. I feel the space between us widening.

'It'll be hard doing so much research,' Tina says. 'I mean who wants to work in the summer?'

Ruby laughs. 'Yes, it will be horribly hard work

chatting up beautiful boys in bathing suits every day, but hey, that's the price one pays for fame.'

They crack up. I back away.

Tina looks at me. 'Come with us, Willa.' She doesn't sound like she means it.

'No, thanks, I have to help my grandmother with something.'

'Testing out new taffies?' Tina says.

Ruby giggles.

'Yeah, something like that.'

'Wait, that reminds me,' Ruby says. 'Come on inside for a minute, Willa.'

The Sivler's kitchen is as spacious as a hotel lobby. On top of the long granite island in the centre of the room, there are water bottles of various sizes and colours, lined up in a row, with a stack of paper cups in front of each.

'We're down to deciding between these two,' Ruby says, pointing to a tall cylindrical blue bottle and a smaller pear-shaped pink bottle. 'Do a taste test will you, Willa?' Ruby says.

'What for?' I say.

'Mommy has to decide on what water to serve our clients at the spa.'

'Isn't the spa for dogs?'

'Yes,' Ruby says, fixing a stray red hair in large, gold-framed mirror. Her fluffy dog, Pookie, runs over. 'Hi, baby.' Ruby picks Pookie up and kisses him on the lips. 'All the top poochie spas have designer water. Mommies and daddies want the best for their babies, right, Pookie?' She rubs noses with the dog and kisses him again.

'This one is ten dollars a bottle,' Tina says, tapping the pink one. 'And this one is twenty.' She holds up the pink bottle to show me. 'Isn't it pretty?'

'Twenty dollars?' I say. 'For a bottle of water? I'm sorry, but I think that's disgusting.'

Tina and Ruby look at me shocked. Pookie whimpers. Ruby holds Pookie tighter to her chest and covers his delicate ears.

'Think of what you could do with twenty dollars,' I say. 'You could probably feed a family for a day, *human beings*, and you're thinking of serving twenty-dollar-a-bottle water to dogs. *Dogs?*'

'*Ugh*.' Ruby looks at me with utter disgust.

'What's wrong with you, Willa?' Tina says angrily.

'Nothing. I'm sorry. I've got to go.'

I bike to the water, heart pounding, head spinning. How could Tina be changing so quickly? Every day she seems more like a clone of Ruby. I need a walk.

Not many people on the beach. Good. It's cloudy, looks like rain. I toss off my sandals, head out to the Spit, breathing in and out, in and out, letting the wind wash it all away. When I reach the tip I stand still for a second and close my eyes. When I open them, I see a dog swimming out of the ocean towards me. I look around me. No one else is here.

The dog reaches the shore, shakes off the water. I recognize it as the dog I saw here with the big crowd yesterday. It's a big golden retriever or is it a Lab or Irish setter – I don't know, I'm not a dog person.

Now the dog is running towards me like it knows me. I'm scared. What if it . . .? Then it reaches me and tackles me to the sand, and before I can catch my breath this big fishy-smelling fur coat of a dog is licking my face, like he's kissing me, like I'm his long-lost owner, who at last, thank goodness, he's finally found. I should be scared, but I'm not.

Salt water is dripping all over my face and all I can do is laugh.

A Mermaid Gift

'Twas one of the charmed days . . .

— Emerson

The dog is licking my cheeks, my nose, my eyebrows. It tickles. I'm laughing. 'Whoa, whoa. Wait a minute. Stop. Who are you? What's your name?' I reach my hands around his neck. There just might be a collar in there somewhere. No, just handfuls of soft smelly gold-brown fur, so thick my hands could get lost in there. He's a big smelly salty polar bear.

'Come on, boy, let me up.' I push the bear dog away and stand up, wiping saliva off my face and brushing the sand off my back as best I can.

The dog is staring at me. He barks, 'Rrrr, rrrr,

rrrr, rrrr,' and wags his tail, 'Rrrr, rrrr, rrrr, rrrr,' like he's trying to tell me something.

Which most likely he is, if I only knew his language.

'Good dog, good dog,' I say, rubbing my hands down his coat. His eyes are big chocolate circles. His nose is wet. He opens his mouth wide, like he's showing me his teeth, and I worry, because isn't that a threatening gesture, but no, wait, he's smiling at me. *The dog is smiling at me*. My heart melts like an ice-cream cone in the Cape Cod sun.

'Where's your owner, buddy?' I look all around, up and down the Spit.

There's a small fishing boat anchored a bit off shore, but I don't see anyone on it.

'Who do you belong to, huh?' I walk up over the dune.

The dog follows me. No one on the bay side either.

I cross back over to the ocean side. The sun breaks through the clouds. Maybe it will be a nice day after all. The dog walks over near the cages where the plover nests are.

'No, buddy,' I say in a stern loud voice. 'Come here.'

I whistle and slap my hand against my thigh like I've seen dog owners do. 'Come here, boy.' At least, I think he's a boy, but I'm certainly not going to investigate.

The dog rises his head up above the seagrass and runs to me.

'Good dog.'

I start back down the beach. Maybe the owner is up in the beach parking lot. At first the dog doesn't move, but then he barks and comes running towards me. I rub his head as a reward. 'Good dog, good dog.'

Good Dog follows behind me and then comes up next to me so we're walking side by side. His fur brushes against my leg and I smile. What a nice dog.

Mariel is coming down the steps with a beach towel ready for a swim.

'Hi, Willa! Who's that? Did you get a *dog*?'

'No. I found him out on the Spit. He came swimming right out of the sea. I didn't see an owner. He doesn't have a collar.'

'Then he's for *you*!' Mare says.

I laugh. 'No. I'm sure he belongs to someone. He's such a beautiful dog.'

'Was there anyone else on the beach?' Mare asks.

'No, just me.'

'Then the sea carried him to you,' Mare says with great certainty. 'My mother told me that if you find a treasure on the beach and you are the only human being in sight, then it is a gift to you from the mermaids.'

I think about how Mare found the snorkel and goggles and how she thought it was a gift, but I don't say anything. I know how much Mare misses her mother. There's no sense debating the silliness of the mermaid idea. Dogs don't just wash up on shore like beach glass or jingle shells or snorkelling gear.

'I'm heading to my grandmother's store,' I say. 'Have a good swim.'

'Thanks,' Mare says. 'Hey, Willa, maybe we can hang together later?'

'Sure,' I say. 'Why don't you come for dinner, say around six?'

'Sounds good.' Mare takes off down the steps.

The dog sits at my feet, looking up at me panting, like, 'So, where are we off to now?'

I pat his head, lean down and stroke his coat. 'You stay here, buddy, OK? I'm sure your owner will be back any minute.'

It's strange, but I almost want to hug this dog. I actually think I wish I could keep him, but no way would my mother ever agree to that.

I get on my bike and pedal off quickly.

I hear the dog barking behind me, but I'm too sad to look back.

No Buts About It

One man's justice is another's injustice;
one man's beauty another's ugliness;
one man's wisdom another's folly.

– Emerson

I bike into town feeling bad about the dog. I look back a few times, but he's not following me. Good. I hope his owner found him. When I pass the ivy-covered Bramble Free Library, a breeze blows and the little green hands wave *Hello, Willa, hello.* I love that old library.

I actually helped save it from closing down. My class hosted fundraising dances in the barn at the inn. The dances were mine and Tina's idea. Our friends, Jessie and Luke, and their band performed. It was fun. The dances didn't raise much money at all, but our guests, the Blazers, had a ball at the Thanksgiving dance, the 'Turkey Tango', and they got wind of the library situation and how much it meant to me and, lo and behold, they became the library's very generous Valentine's donor. That was the night JFK and I danced in the barn by firelight and he gave me the heart-shaped locket.

I need to talk with him. Where has he been?

I pass the movie theatre, the two-for-one tourist T-shirt shop, Fancy's Fish Market, and Wickstrom's jewellers, where JFK bought the locket. If he doesn't call me back today, I'm biking over to his house tonight.

My hairdresser, Jo, is in the window of her salon, Hairs to You. There are tall silver buckets of pink and white stargazer lilies out front of Delilah's florist. I can't resist. I stop and breathe them in. Hmmm, beautiful.

When I get to Sweet Bramble Books, the bells above the door jangle a greeting, and the smell of chocolate, mint and taffy swirl up to my nose, *Hello*. Nana is at the counter weighing individual cellophane bags of penny candy for a family with several children. The father is watching the numbers on the scales and the mother is searching for something in her pocketbook. One of the kids, he looks about three years old, backs over to the Swedish-fish bin, checking to make sure his parents are still distracted, and then with this big grin on his face is just about to stick his hand in the fish when Nana calls out, without even looking, 'Use the scoop, young man. Thank you.'

The kid jumps, nearly pees his pants scared, like *How did she see me?* I giggle quietly. Nana's got X-ray vision when it comes to kids messing with her Swedish-fish bin. Nana looks over at me and waves. Scamp comes to greet me. I bend down and scratch him around his ears as he likes, but instead of rolling on his back so I can rub his belly, Scamp barks and sniffs my fingers. He probably smells the dog from the beach. I hope the dog found his owner by now.

Over on the book side of the store, Dr Swaminathan, my English teacher at Bramble Academy, is just finishing with a customer. That's right . . . Nana said he'd be working here part-time this summer. She said she'd be glad to have someone so highly knowledgeable about books. Nana is the candy expert. Gramp was the book lover in the family. He owned the town bookstore and then, when he and Nana married, they combined their businesses into Sweet Bramble Books, my notion of the perfect store.

'If you enjoy the book, there's a sequel due out in January,' Dr Swammy is saying to the customer. 'Let me know what you think, Mrs Nevett. I'll be interested to hear.'

The lady thanks him and leaves.

It feels strange to see another man standing there behind the counter in my grandfather's spot, in the bookstore Gramp loved so much. I can feel Gramp's spirit here. I hope I always will. And I know Gramp would approve of Dr Swaminathan. Dr Swammy loves books the way Gramp loved books. Nana and I joke that Gramp's probably up in heaven right now, starting book clubs and making sure God reads the 'good ones'.

'Hello, Willa,' Dr Swaminathan says. 'How's your summer going?'

'Great,' I say. 'How was India?'

'I enjoyed spending time with my family,' he

says, 'but I was saddened by the spread of the water crisis.'

'The water crisis?'

Dr Swaminathan shakes his head. 'Very, very dirty water.'

I lean on the counter and Dr Swammy explains how water-borne diseases are threatening the lives of thousands, maybe millions of people.

'The Ganges is poisoned,' he says, 'and yet people still drink from it. They scoop it up in their hands like you and I turn on a faucet in our kitchen. And the problem doesn't end there. The polluted water is also used for crops and so it affects the food supply as well. All across India,' he says sadly. 'Wells are closed, pumps are locked. People are dying of thirst.'

People are dying because they don't have water. In this day and age? How can that be? 'What can I do?' I say, ready to help.

Dr Swammy smiles. He tells me about an organization he's affiliated with that raises money to bring in water-treatment equipment and dig for new wells. As he talks, I think maybe I've found my new service project for the summer. I think about the fancy water bottles we have at the inn and the designer water at the pet spa. Something's very wrong with this picture. I want to investigate this issue further online later.

Dr Swaminathan asks what I'm reading.

'I haven't started our required class list yet,' I say, 'but don't worry, I'll get to it in August.'

Dr Swammy laughs. 'I wasn't worried at all.'

I tell Dr Swammy about the skinny-punch books and some of the titles Mrs Saperstone suggested for me.

'Very nice selections,' Dr Swaminathan says. He stares at me for a second. 'Willa, do you know . . . is Mrs Saperstone staying in Bramble for the summer?'

There's an unfamiliar sweetness in the tone of Dr Swammy's voice. I look at him and he looks away as if embarrassed, or no, shy – maybe he's shy.

'I want to consult with her about a writing contest I'm thinking of starting,' he says, not looking at me while he's talking.

Beep-beep-beep. My Cape Cupid radar registers in my brain. Dr Swammy likes Mrs Saperstone!

Of course. I've seen them sitting together at BUC. They'd be perfect for each other. They're both single, about the same age, they both love books. *Perfect.*

If I may brag for a moment, I do have a stellar reputation for matchmaking. First I hooked up my mother and Sam. I should have won a gold medal for that one. Even though Stella Havisham had a booming business planning other people's weddings, my mother had written off love for herself. She had been so broken-hearted over my birth father's death. Stupid hot-air balloon. What was he thinking about anyway?

Next I played Cupid for Nana and Gramp Tweed. He ran a bookstore; she ran Clancy's Candies. Books and candy, my two favourite things. Nana and Mr Tweed, my two favourite people. It was a no-brainer, truly. I invited them to a picnic at my house and *boing*, it was love at first bite (of the picnic food I mean, no vampires in Bramble that I know of).

My most recent match was Sulamina Mum and Riley Truth. All I did was coax Mum into writing a letter to her long-lost high-school sweetheart – it was no easy task; she fought me on it – but finally Mum took a leapfrog leap of faith and wrote Riley a letter and *boing*, that letter hit home better than that bare-butt baby's bow and arrow. I'm now a firm believer in being a 'leaper'. Sometimes you've just got to close your eyes and leap right over the scary part to get to the thing you want.

'You should go to the Bramble Library tonight,' I say. 'Mrs Saperstone is doing a programme on good beach reads. The Red Hat ladies were talking about it this—'

'The Red Hat whos?'

'This cool group of ladies who are staying at the inn, but enough about them, back to Mrs Saperstone. It starts at seven. There'll be iced tea and refreshments. I know she'd love to see you.'

'Really?' Dr Swaminathan says.

I can't tell for sure, but he looks like he's blushing.

'Absolutely,' I nod my head definitively. 'Oh, and, maybe you'd like to take her some candy? I know Mrs Saperstone loves those chocolate-covered cranberries Nana makes.'

*

Back over on the candy side of Sweet Bramble Books, Nana comes towards me with her arms wide open. 'Give me a hug, shmug.'

I tell Nana what I found out about the new saltwater taffy section at Ghelfi's. 'You can't compete with their variety,' I say, 'so we need a different strategy.'

'OK, good,' Nana says, looking around the store for spies, rubbing her hands together, lowering her voice to a whisper. 'Hit me with it.'

'I was thinking . . . you know how you get those little messages inside fortune cookies and how much fun that can be?'

Nana nods her head.

'Well, what if we tied happy thoughts around the taffies, like they do around Hershey's Kisses. Sort of add to the value of the purchase? Create a new candy buzz?'

Nana claps her hands all excited. 'I like it!'

'I can write the messages,' I say, 'no problem. All you'd need to do is print them out and cut and—'

'Brilliant!' Nana says, hugging me. 'I tell you, Willa Havisham Gracemore, you've got good candy genes. Good book sense and candy smarts. Sweet Bramble Books will be yours some day.'

Outside, I get on my bike, feeling proud that I can help Nana. I'll start writing those taffy tags today. It will be fun.

Passing the town green, I spot the dog from the beach. He looks up at me and barks and runs towards me like he's been waiting for me. I keep biking.

He's following me.

I turn the corner towards home and, sure enough, the dog follows me up the driveway to the Bramblebriar Inn. I can hear him panting behind me.

Maybe if I ignore him, he'll go away.

'Willa! Come say hello,' my mother calls to me. She's sitting on the front porch with Katie Caldor and Mrs Caldor, and four pretty girls, probably Katie's bridesmaids, most likely going over last-minute wedding details.

Mrs Caldor is wearing a stunning pale blue sundress with matching hat. The Caldors are known for exquisite taste in fashion. They own the chain of Caldor Creek clothing stores that started right here on Cape Cod.

I start up the steps. I hear the dog following me.

Go. Go away.

'What a cute dog!' Katie Caldor says and, as if on cue, the dog bounds up to the wicker table, knocking over the pitcher of lemonade right on to Mrs Caldor's lap.

She jumps up, horrified.

'Oh, Vivian, I'm so sorry,' my mother says, peeling a lemon rind off of Mrs Caldor's beautiful dress. 'Willa, run and get a towel and some club soda.'

After the Caldors leave, I bring the dog a dish of water. He laps it up gratefully and then sprawls out under a shady tree, big brown eyes looking up sheepish.

'That's the dog that defecated on the beach yesterday, isn't it?' Stella says.

'Mom, give him a break. He's just a dog.' And then, I know she'll say 'no', but I always say you've got to be a leaper and so I take a leap: 'Mom, do you think he could stay here for a while until we find the owner? I'll make up signs and post them around town—'

'Absolutely not,' she says. 'In fact, please go ask Sam to call Animal Control or town hall or whoever one calls about these things.'

'Mom, that's not fair.'

'You heard me Willa.' My mother lowers her voice as some guests walk by.

'But, Mom—'

'No buts about it, Willa. I don't want a dog traipsing through my inn.'

My temper flares. 'Well, it's my home too, and you better get ready for no *mutts* about it, because the Sivlers are opening up a pampered-pet spa next door and *dogs* are going to be our new neighbours.'

13

Salty from the Sea

*Nothing great was ever achieved without
enthusiasm.*

— Emerson

I storm into the inn to look for Sam. He's out in
the vegetable garden.

His eyes smile when he sees me. Sam is always
happy to see me.

I burst into tears and tell him what's going on.

'Well,' Sam says, taking off his gloves, 'first let's
see this dog.'

We walk out front to the big oak tree. The dog
is sound asleep. Sam kneels on the grass beside
him and gently pets the dog. The dog opens his
eyes. He looks at Sam and then he looks at me.

I pet him and he licks my hand.

'What a gorgeous golden,' Sam says.

'So he's a golden retriever?'

'Yep. I had one when I was growing up.'

'What was your dog's name, Dad?'

'Henry.'

I laugh. 'Where did you get the name Henry?'

'I don't know,' Sam says, laughing, 'but I'm sure it made perfect sense at the time.' Sam rubs his hands through fur. The dog rolls on his back and lifts up his paw like he wants to shake Sam's hand. Sam shakes his paw and laughs. 'Good dog.'

'What happened to Henry?' I ask.

'He died of old age when I was in college. He lived a good long life though, old Henry did. Ruthie and I . . . we loved that dog.'

'Speaking of Aunt Ruthie,' I say, 'I think I've got everything planned for the wedding.' I tell Sam about the idea to hold the ceremony in the labyrinth. It seems only fitting that Sam's sister should get married here. The labyrinth is Sam's creation. It's a circular garden path. You enter between two shrubs and follow the narrow walkway, looping in towards the centre, out towards the border, circling round and round until you reach the stone bench in the middle. Sam says walking the labyrinth is a spiritual thing for him. Sam has planted perennial flowers and berried bushes all along the borders so that there's always something beautiful blooming as you walk. It's funny though – when I walk the labyrinth, I don't focus on the flowers at all. I walk and breathe and wait to hear whatever comes up inside me.

My mother comes down the steps to join us. 'Have you reported this yet?'

Sam turns and looks at my mother. She folds her arms across her chest.

'I was just about to do that, Stella,' Sam says. 'Such a beautiful dog.'

'Shake my hand, boy,' I say, and sure enough he does.

'So smart, so smart,' I say. I look at my mother. She isn't melting a bit.

'Oh, and watch this, Mom,' I say, 'he *smiles*.' I smile a great big jack-o'-lantern toothy smile at the dog. 'Come on, buddy, smile. Smile.'

The dog looks at my mother and barks.

'Well, if you aren't going to call someone, I will,' Mom says. 'This dog could have fleas or ticks or rabies or who knows what.' She walks up the steps and into the inn.

I stay with my dog from the sea. It's peaceful, just him and me.

Sam leaves and comes back with some leftovers from last night's dinner. The dog sniffs the roast beef and turns away.

'I think he prefers seafood,' I say.

Sam goes in and comes back with a bowl of dry cereal. This is more to the dog's liking. The Millers are walking up the driveway. They come over to see the dog. Mike the mailman comes and I go to get our mail. Two postcards for me! One from Mum and Riley from Disney World. One from Suzanna Jubilee and Simon on their honeymoon in Italy. 'Venice is spectacular,' Suzy says. 'We ride the ganolas every day. And you should see the boys here, Willa. Bellissimo, bellissimo. We're coming to visit you in August! I'll bring pictures. Ciao, bella bébé, hugs and kisses, Suzy-Jube.'

Mum says, 'We met Mickey and Minnie, took a ride in Cindy's pumpkin and had breakfast with Pooh. The fireworks show was spectacular, but couldn't hold a sparkler to Cape fireworks on the fourth of July. I miss Bramble. Hope you like the new minister. Give my love to everyone. And please tell Stella and Sam to plan a visit. Riley and I would love to show you some Southern hospitality. Love, Mum.'

There's a letter addressed to the Bramblebriar Inn, 'Attention Rosie'. I note the return address. It's from Mrs Chickles Blazer at their California zipcode. They own at least three mansions in this country and a chateau in Paris too.

Hmmmm. I wonder why Mama B is writing to Rosie? Oh, I know. I bet it's about the wedding cake Rosie made for Suzy-Jube's wedding. Mama B nearly split a seam raving about that cake. She said it was the best she'd ever eaten. 'Give me your phone number, honey. Papa B and I are going to make you famous!'

The Animal Control truck pulls up. A man gets out; says his name is Mark Sweeney. He asks me where I found the dog. I tell him as much as I can recall. Mr Sweeney approaches the dog slowly and gently puts a harness around him.

'Where are you taking him?' I ask, feeling like I'm going to cry.

'Bramble Animal Shelter.'

'Where's that?'

'On Mill Road, across from the waste-treatment plant,' he says, then laughs. 'Not much of a location, but we just planted some flowers out front.'

I know where the waste-treatment plant is. I passed it on the way to Mariel's when I followed her home from the library one day. I wanted to see where she lived. 'What are you going to do with him?' I ask in a very stern voice like, you'd better treat him well.

Sam comes over next to me and puts his hand on my shoulder.

'We'll scan him for a chip,' Mr Sweeney says. He explains that many pet owners now have a microchip implanted in their dogs and cats for easy identification if they get lost.

'We'll check him for fleas, give him a bath. This one's a smelly guy, huh, boy?'

'He's just salty from the sea,' I say, defending my dog.

'We'll give him a rabies shot. Check him over. Be sure he's not injured. If he is, we'll take him to the vet; otherwise we'll just kennel him and hold him for five days.'

'How do you try to find the owner?' Sam asks.

'We'll post a photo on our website and hope for a call.'

'What happens after five days?' I say, all worried. What if they put him to sleep?

'It's Bramble town policy that after the sixth day, if the owner doesn't show, we get the animal ready for adoption. We make sure it's spayed or neutered and flea-free, and run through a behavioural test.'

'*Adoption?*' I say. I look at Sam. He nods and smiles reassuringly.

I feel hope rising inside me like a balloon. 'You mean if no one comes in a week, we could adopt him?'

'Sure,' Mr Sweeney says. 'And I hope you will. You'd have to pay a fee, of course, and we'd have to come do a home inspection, a background check—'

'A background check?' Sam says.

'Well, basically, we'd talk with your neighbours and make sure there's no history of animal cruelty.'

'We love animals,' I say, already auditioning for the role of 'Mom'. 'I promise I would take excellent care of him . . . feed him, walk him, groom him . . . Salty would be the most pampered and loved dog in Bramble.'

'Well that sounds fine,' Mr Sweeney says, 'but for now, I've got to take this guy with me. See if his owners show up.'

My eyes fill with tears. *Don't show up, don't show up. This is my dog now.* I hug salty dog and whisper, 'Don't worry, boy, you'll be OK. I'll come visit you tomorrow.'

Up in my room, I take out my journal and pour out fast what's happening.

I might adopt a dog! He's already mine. In my heart, I know he is. Mare's right. He came to me. From the mermaids, straight out of the sea. Could Salty have fallen overboard from that boat anchored in the bay? No. That would have been a very long way to swim. Dogs don't like to swim that far, right? I have no idea. I don't know much about dogs at all. Except that I love this one. And Sam and I have a whole week to work on Mother. Maybe when she sees how much we both want . . .

When I finish writing, I take out my bag of saltwater taffy. I'm in the mood for peppermint. I open a smooth white and red striped candy and pop it in my mouth. That reminds me. The messages for Nana's 'taffy tags'. I like this idea. I should get a patent on it or something, as Tina would say.

I wonder how Tina and Ruby's book is coming along.

I grab a notebook and pen. Let's see . . . taffy, taffy . . .

Eat taffy. Be happy.
A taffy a day keeps the troubles away.
One taffy's good; two is better.
Don't worry. Be taffy.
Sand sneakers, taffy teeth – Welcome to Cape Cod.

I laugh and put the notebook aside. Nana's going to love these. Nana would be so happy for me if I could adopt Salty. Why does Stella have to be so mean?

I look at my short stack of skinny-punch books, scanning the titles. Which to choose next? *The*

Hundred Dresses by Eleanor Estes, *The Whipping Boy* by Sid Fleischman. My eyes land on *Love That Dog* by Sharon Creech. I know that author. She won the Newbery Medal for *Walk Two Moons*. I open *Dog* and start reading.

When I get to the line about the 'yellow dog', I smile.

I'm going to have a yellow dog too.

Soon – I just know I will.

14

Stupid Baseball

The only way to have a friend is to be one.

— Emerson

Mariel comes at six for dinner. With her deep
brown eyes, glistening skin and long black ringlety
hair, she's stunning in a simple denim skirt and
tank top. She has on the beach-glass necklace,
with the brown, blue and green pattern she was
wearing the day I discovered that she and Joseph
were friends. We all ran into one another outside
Nana's store. It was awkward. I was jealous when
she got the role of Emily in *Our Town* and JFK got
the male lead and they kissed in the play, but JFK
insisted that he and Mare are just friends.

'Am I too early?' Mare says.

'No, you're right on time. Come on in. My

mom's out shopping and my dad's running the kitchen tonight, so it'll be just us.'

I worked out the menu with Sam ahead of time. Barbecued chicken, potato salad, sliced tomatoes and green beans.

'Hello, Mariel,' Sam says, draining a pot at the sink and then moving back to the sizzling pan on the burner. 'Welcome. How's your summer going?'

'Great, Mr Gracemore, thanks.'

'Can we expect to see you in any more productions this summer?' Sam asks.

'I want to audition for Maid Marian in Robin Hood,' Mare says, 'but the Wellfleet Playhouse is out of biking distance, so we'll see.'

That must be the audition she was talking to JFK about at the baseball field. I sure hope he's not auditioning. Aren't Robin Hood and Maid Marian in love? I'm certain there would be kissing.

Something steams up on the stove and Sam turns. 'I'm sorry . . . back to work. Why don't you girls fill your plates and sit out at the picnic table by the pond? It's a perfect evening for alfresco dining. And I've got the wickets set up for croquet.'

'That sounds nice,' Mare says. 'Thanks for having me over, Mr Gracemore.'

We fill our plates and head outside. I tell Mare to 'duck' when we pass by the dining-room window. 'If the Red Hats spot us they'll want to talk all night or, worse still, join us.'

Mare laughs. 'I like them. I plan on being a Red Hat when I'm older. Red hat, red shoes, red everything. I want to live life *big* and have some fun. Don't you, Willa?'

'Absolutely.'

We talk about the bird thing. We talk about books. Mare says she's reading *Esperanza Rising* by Pam Muñoz Ryan, and highly recommends it. I ask her how long it is. I tell her I'll try it when I'm off my diet. Mare laughs when I tell her about the skinny-punch books. She says she wants to try that too.

'I'll give you my Willa's Pix list,' I say.

'Where did you get that idea from?' she asks.

I tell her how I went to Saratoga, New York, with Tina and her family on a summer vacation and we visited the famous racecourse there. Local kids do a daily 'Kids' Pix', listing their favourite horses in each of the races that day. That seems like so long ago now. Something tells me that if Tina had to pick a friend to go with her this summer she would pick Ruby.

I look at Mare. She's looking out at the pond, enjoying her food, enjoying being here. Such a different place than the ugly motel she lives in.

I'm glad Mare's here. I like her, a lot. I can tell we're going to be good friends, but right now I'm hoping she won't stay too long. I want to see JFK tonight.

'I can only hang out until seven,' I say. 'I have to go somewhere.'

She's your friend, Willa, just tell her the truth. No . . . what if she wants to come too?

'Oh, sure,' Mare says. 'I need to leave soon anyway. I promised Papa I'd pick up some things at the market.'

'How is your father? And Nico and Sofia?'

Mariel's father is in a wheelchair. JFK said he was injured in a work-related accident. I'm not sure how. Nico and Sofia are twins – two years old, I think. I don't ask Mare about her mother. I want to, but it feels too personal. I'm hoping she'll talk about her some day though. JFK said Mrs Sanchez is an actress off pursuing her 'big break', with Mariel's blessing, if you can believe it. Mare told JKF her mother was like a bird who would die if her wings were clipped. Well, that might be so, but it seems to me a mother bird shouldn't fly off and leave her babies, no matter how talented she is.

We take our dishes into the kitchen. Sam gives Mare a container of fresh-from-the-oven chocolate-chip cookies to take home to her family. When Mare leaves, I go upstairs and fix my hair, brush my teeth and put on some lipgloss and perfume. I put some cookies in a bag, stick it in the basket of my bike, and head toward JFK's, taking a different route so I won't run into Mariel at the market.

As I pass the grey clapboard Bramble Beach Association building, the parking lot is full. A sign reads: 'Important Meeting Tonight, 7 p.m.'

That's funny, I don't remember Mom and Sam talking about a meeting tonight. We belong to the BBA. All the people who own homes in this area do, a couple of hundred families I think it is. We pay yearly dues for beach maintenance and landscaping and other stuff. In the summer, there are softball games, craft classes and movies for kids. Card games and things for adults. Nana likes the Thursday night square dances. The big event is the fourth of July Field Day, coming up next week.

I wonder what the meeting's about? I wheel my bike into the rack and go inside.

Ruby Sivler's father is at the front of the room. There's Tina's father, Mr Belle. There's the lady who owns the huge white house with the swimming pool right at the entrance to Sandy Beach. And several people I recognize as Ruby and Tina's neighbours. The 'boat crowd' as Sam would say.

'It's high time we took back our beach,' Mr Sivler is saying. 'First we've got intruders trespassing on our beach more and more each summer, and now the best part of the Spit is roped off for *birds*. I don't know about you, but I work hard all week. I want to enjoy my beach on the weekends. There's something wrong with this picture, people.'

There's lots of clapping.

'We need to protect our investment,' Tina's father says. 'And we need to take action quickly.

The sand on the Spit is slipping away like the proverbial hourglass. First it's a few beach towels and a boat anchored here and there next thing you know, they'll be pitching tents and acting like they live here.'

There's a commotion throughout the room.

'As president of the BBA,' Mr Sivler says, 'I've taken the liberty of developing a system for preserving our rights and policing what we're entitled to.'

Mr Sivler explains that every Bramble family who has 'legal deeded rights' to the beach will be given a small white flag with a number on it. He holds one up and waves it to show how simple the idea is. 'Each certified BBA member family, whose annual dues are paid, will be assigned a flag with a number. 'When you're at the beach, just post your flag in the sand next to you. Then we'll all know who belongs here and who doesn't.'

'How we gonna enforce that?' someone shouts out.

'Good question,' Mr Sivler says. 'We've hired three retired police officers to patrol the beach and guard the entrances to the parking lot. They will approach unfamiliar people and ask to see their flag. If the party cannot produce a flag, they will be escorted off the beach.'

There's a rumble of 'good's and 'that's right's and lots of heads nodding.

I feel uneasy inside. Something's not right here.

'But this system will only work if we all participate,' Mr Sivler says. 'We must be vigilant. If you are on the beach and see a party you don't recognize, ask them to produce their flag. Or, if you are uncomfortable approaching strangers, which is perfectly understandable in the world we live in today, just talk to one of the patrol officers and they'll take care of the situation.'

'The bottom line is this,' the lady who hires the lifeguards says, 'you either belong on this beach or you don't. We're just protecting what's ours.'

You've got to be kidding me. They sound like a bunch of toddlers crying, 'Stay away from my sand-box or I'm going to tell my Mommy!' Maybe that's why Tina was asking Mariel who she was with on the beach, implying that she didn't belong there. Poor Mariel bikes miles from her crummy motel-room home to swim at this beach. She's not harming anything. I think the flag thing is a stupid idea and I have half a mind to speak my piece about the beach, but it will be dark soon and I've got my priorities in order. Boyfriend? Beach? Boyfriend? Beach? That's easy.

When I get to Joseph's house, there he is, sitting on the steps talking to Mariel. *What is she doing here?* I drop my bike on the lawn and walk towards them.

'Hey, Willa,' Mariel says, standing up to go. 'See ya later, Joe. Sorry you can't do Robin Hood, but I'm happy for you. Have fun. Send me a postcard, OK? I've got to pick up milk. See you guys later.'

I walk up the stairs. JFK smiles. 'Hi,' he says.

'Where have you been?' I say. 'Why haven't you called? I've left you tons of messages.'

'I know. I'm sorry. Stuff came up . . .'

'What stuff?' I'm angry. *What stuff could be more important than your girlfriend?*

'Baseball.'

Of course.

'Guess what,' he says all excited. 'My dad's friend, the sports editor down at the paper, got me a gig working at the Florida Dolphins training camp!'

'In *Florida*?'

'Yes! Isn't that great? I can stay with my grandparents and . . .'

'When?' I say, my heart sinking into my stomach.

'I'm leaving Friday, I think. As soon as Dad gets my ticket and Mom finishes packing me up.' His face is glowing.

'For how long?'

'The whole month.'

'Wow,' I say, 'that's great.'

'I know,' JFK says, 'can you believe it!'

We talk for a while, small stuff. He's so happy, I don't tell him how I truly feel. Not after I spoilt his joy about the sailing boat. I'm not going to rain on his baseball parade too. *It's only a month. Deal with it, Willa. But it's summer vacation and he's my boyfriend. Right, but he's your friend too. See how happy he is? Be happy for him. He'd be happy for you. Stupid baseball. Soccer is a much better sport.*

'It's dark,' Joseph says. 'I'll bike you home.'

When we get to the inn, all the lights are lit up and someone's playing the piano. Next door, the soon-to-be pet spa is all lit up too. Several workers are inside, hanging curtains, opening boxes, filling shelves. There's a sign out front: Grand Opening July lst. That's this Saturday. My first solo wedding day. And I wanted JFK to come. I try not to be upset.

We sit up on the old stone fence. JFK inches in closer to me. Crickets are chirping, a firefly flits past, the sky is brimming with stars. *Stop showing off, Nature.*

Joseph takes my hand, twines his fingers through mine. 'Hey,' he says in a sweet, soft voice. 'Why so quiet?'

'No reason.'

He touches my chin, turns it towards him, and then he kisses me. He smells faintly of sun lotion – he was probably sailing today. We kiss until I hear the Red Hats laughing and hollering and hooting it up coming up the street from town. Those ladies are having way too much fun just coming from the library. Their laughter is contagious. It makes us laugh too.

'I'll call you tomorrow,' JFK says. He jumps down from the fence and then reaches his hands around my waist to help me down. We kiss again, so what if the Red Hats see.

I'm too wired to write in my journal. My mind is spinning. I can't sleep. I go up on the widow's walk. Long ago, Cape Cod wives would pace back and forth on these rooftop perches, staring out to sea, hoping to spot their husband's boat sailing safely home to harbour. Unfortunately the whaling life was a treacherous one, and many men died at sea. Thus the name 'widow's walk'. I check out the sky, spot the North Star and the dippers, let the air whoosh against my face, then go back to my room, still restless.

I reach for *Locomotion* by Jacqueline Woodson. There are three books by her in my summer stack. I pull out my taffy and start reading:

This whole book's a poem 'cause every time I try to tell the whole story my mind goes Be Quiet!

*

The taffy wrappers pile up. I'm finished in an hour. Wow, can this lady write. I love the 'voice'. English-teacher Sam says you can teach people a lot of things about writing – plotting, pacing, characterization – but voice, that's something of a mystery. Sam says a writer either has it or she hasn't. Jacqueline Woodson has it.

When I snuggle under the covers, I close my eyes and the movie starts in my mind. JFK and I kissing on the old stone fence. At least we have a few more days. At least he's not heading out to sea for who knows how long on a whale hunt. Stupid baseball. Then I picture Salty Dog smiling at me and wonder how he's doing.

15

Bad, Bad Bottle

*Beware when the great God lets loose
a thinker on this planet.*

— **Emerson**

When I finish work Tuesday morning I bike fast
as I can to Mill Road, holding my breath as I pass
the garbage treatment plant. Gosh does that place
stink.

There are red, white and blue petunias planted
in a flag pattern outside Bramble Animal Shelter.
Mr Sweeney smiles when he sees me.

'I had a feeling I'd be seeing you today,' he
says.

'Did the owner come?' I ask, heart pounding.
Please, please say no.

'No,' he says, smiling. 'Want to see him?'

'Yes!' I follow Mr Sweeney back into the kennel area. Past a row of cats who peer sadly and quietly out at me, then into the dog section, where they make more of a ruckus to get your attention. I look at each animal as we pass, smiling and silently saying, *Don't worry, keep hopeful, someone will adopt you, I'm sure.* And then I see my dog.

'Salty!'

Mr Sweeney unlocks the cage. Salty jumps towards me. I kneel and hug him tight. He smells different, like soap. 'So you got a bath, huh, boy?'

Mr Sweeney gives me some treats for Salty and lets me take him out on a leash in the backyard. Salty seems so happy to see me. I stay for an hour.

'Be back tomorrow!'

I'm over in Mariel's neighbourhood. Maybe she's home. I bike past the trailer park, then I see the sign 'Oceanview Inn: TOURISTS WELCOME'.

The Oceanview Inn is a dirty, dumpy, run-down motel that hasn't welcomed a tourist in a long time. It's an inch up from a homeless shelter, yards down from an apartment building, miles away from being a real house.

Poor people who can't afford the cost of an apartment here on Cape Cod rent rooms here by the month. Mariel's whole family lives in one room – room number five. Two people are arguing loudly in number seven; a baby's crying in number six. As I approach the Sanchez's door I hear singing. It's a young woman's voice; it must be Mariel. The melody is familiar, but the words are in Spanish. What a beautiful voice.

I stand there listening for a moment. When I knock, the singing stops.

I hear giggling, Nico and Sofia, and then Mare opens the door.

'Willa!' She seems confused and embarrassed. She moves me outside, closing the door behind us. I can hear the twins giggling louder like this is some sort of game.

'What are you doing here?' Mare says, not in a happy tone.

'I was in the neighbourhood and I thought I'd stop by.'

'Why didn't you call first?' she says.

'I'm sorry.' But inside I'm thinking, you stop by my house and you don't call first.

'What are you doing around here?' she asks.

'The animal shelter up the road,' I say. 'I went to visit the dog I found.'

'Your dog,' Mare says, her face brightening.

'I hope so,' I say.

'No, he's yours,' Mare says, confident as one of those court judges on TV. 'I told you, if the sea sends you something on an empty beach, it is a gift from the mermaids.'

'What are you doing today?' I say, trying to change the subject. I feel sort of hurt that she isn't inviting me in.

'I have to watch the kids. My dad's working.'

'I'd like to meet them,' I say, 'Nico and Sofia.'

Mare stares at me for a second like she's considering this.

'What's wrong?' I say.

'It's just that they get all excited about meeting new people and then they keep asking when they're going to see them again.'

'Well, no problem there,' I say. 'I think they'll be seeing a lot of me.'

Mare smiles. I smile back. We don't say it, but I know we're both thinking the same thing. We're going to be good friends. Her brother and sister will see me again.

When Mare opens the door, Sofia and Nico are hiding under the bed. 'Ooh, where have those little kittens gone,' Mare says, and we hear the giggling. 'Miaow, miaow, miaow,' they say, crawling out. Mare introduces us. We have animal crackers and apple juice. We play Candy Land, my favourite game when I was their age. When I tell Nico and Sofia that my grandmother owns a candy store, their eyes bug large like I'm a rock star on MTV.

'I'll bring you some candy next time I come. What kind do you like?'

'Bring it all!' Nico says.

'Mucho, Mucho,' Sofia says, and they roll on the floor, giggling.

When I get home, I go up to my room and look over the plans for Ruthie's wedding. The weather is supposed to be nice on Saturday. We'll do the ceremony in the labyrinth. There will only be a few guests and the service will be short, so we can all stand in a circle around Ruthie and Spruce. I think they should sit on the stone bench in the centre. Yes, we'll all be there in the inner circle, while they process in through the labyrinth. Sam has helped me pick some readings and Ruthie's favourite poem. It's the one by Robert Frost about 'The Road Not Taken . . .' I'm still not sure about music. When we hold formal wedding ceremonies at BUC, Mrs Bellimo belts out songs from the choir loft. We can't do that in the labyrinth. I ask Sam. He says you can't go wrong with the Beatles. He gives me his Beatles CD. I pick out 'Let It Be'. Now I just need to find someone to sing it. I think of Mariel singing this morning. I wonder if she'd be willing?

JFK calls and asks if I want to bike out to Woods Hole.

'I'll pack lunch,' I say. Tuna-fish sandwiches and Cape Cod Potato Chips, peaches, brownies and two bottled waters.

We take the Sea of Shining Sea Trail out to Woods Hole, through a shady area with lots of wild flowers, out along a beautiful strip of the coastline, past Nobska Lighthouse, standing tall.

Woods Hole is a cool town. Scientists from all over the world come here to conduct ocean research. We lock our bikes on a rack in the centre park area and walk through town. They're feeding the harbour seals at the research aquarium at the end of the street. I remember Nana taking me here in summer when I was little and came to stay with her while Mom was busy with her wedding-planning business. There's a 'please touch' water box inside the building. I'll never forget the first time I picked up a live starfish, and a horseshoe crab, and a lobster, all slimy and wriggling in my hand.

We walk back to the park, check out the old sundial in the centre. JFK takes a long drink from the orange bottle with the black top he has hooked on his belt loop. We find a grassy spot in the shade and I take out our lunch.

'You should get a reusable water container,' JFK says, holding up one of my 'Only the Best for Bramblebriar Guests' bottles and turning it around in the sun. 'These plastic bottles are wickedly bad for the planet. I did a science project at my old school in Minnesota. Americans buy like 30 billion of these a year.'

'At least they get recycled,' I say.

'Actually only about a fifth of them do. The other eighty per cent end up in landfills. The plastic never breaks down. It's awful for the earth and animals, especially birds. They ingest it and choke and die. Not to mention the oil.'

'What to do you mean?'

'I think I remember it takes something like 50 million gallons of oil a year to make these plastic bottles, just in America alone. And then there's the carbon-dioxide pollution made during the manufacturing.'

I have excellent taste in boyfriends if I do say so myself. Not only is Joseph handsome, kind, poetic, and smart, but he thinks about bigger issues like stopping the war and saving the planet. I hold up my bottle. 'Bad, bad bottle,' I say in a stern voice. JFK laughs. 'No, seriously,' I say, 'I'm going to get a refillable bottle like yours, Joseph. Do they come in green?'

He laughs. 'Yeah, they come in lots of colours.'

'Mine will have to be green, for Bramblebriar, of course.'

After lunch we get ice cream and sit with our legs dangling off the pier, watching the boats come in and out. I turn just as Joseph is pointing to something, and his cone bumps into my nose. He wipes off the ice cream, then kisses my nose.

We bike home, wind sailing through my hair, sun beating on my face. It's a perfect date on a perfect summer day. Neither of us mentions Florida. Bad, bad baseball.

JFK has to go somewhere with his family. I bike into town to tell Nana about the taffy tags I've come up with so far. Dr Swaminathan and Mrs Saperstone are coming out of a restaurant. They are laughing, all happy about something. Dr Swammy opens the door of his car and Mrs S gets in, just as I'm pulling up behind them. I don't call out. Let those young lovebirds alone is what Nana would say. Dr Swammy has a bumper sticker: *Think Global. Start Local.* I think about that for a minute.

Nana loves the taffy-tag lines. She writes them

down. 'I'll get these printed up right away,' she says. I get some mints for Mom, chocolate walnut fudge for Sam, and me . . . I'm in the mood for fish. I 'use the scoop' and shovel up a bag of those yummy red gummy guppies.

Back at the inn, I help with the cocktail social hour. I cut veggies and scoop out fresh dill dip into a bowl. I light little yellow candles out on the sun porch, turn on some music, carry out the fresh fruit and cheese platter, mingle around chatting with the guests.

The Red Hats are off to dinner at Wimpy's in Osterville and then karaoke night at the British Beer Company in Falmouth. They've been practising some hot numbers all day. They show me their red boas and test out a few lines of a song from the musical *Chicago*. Oh, I wish Chickles Blazer was here. Mama B would love these gals!

Up in my room, I check out my books. Tonight I'm in the mood for comedy. Mrs S was surprised that I hadn't read *The Whipping Boy* by Sid Fleischman. Great illustration on the cover. I plop down on my bed, dig into the fish, and start reading.

Mrs S was right. This is a hoot.

I brush my teeth, all red from the fish, and think about what I'm going to wear for Ruthie and Spruce's wedding. They're coming Thursday. No need for a rehearsal Friday. It will be such a simple affair. I look through my closet, not sure what to wear. I don't know how formal Ruthie's going to be. I pull out the dress I wore at Suzy-Jube's wedding. It's pale yellow, the colour of sherbet, silky, with a poofy skirt that swirled when I danced. I felt like a princess in this dress. I was Suzy's maid of honour. I try it on. Yep, it looks good. I hang it back up and pull out the dress I wore the following day for Mum and Riley's wedding. I was Mum's maid of honour too. This is a simple linen sundress, pale pink. It looked so nice with my silver locket and little silver dangling earrings. I try on the dress. Yep, it looks good too.

I pick up *The Hundred Dresses* by Eleanor Estes, written more than sixty years ago. I leaf through it before I start. There are black and white illustrations throughout, with bursts of water-colours here and there. It's about a girl named Wanda who wears the same old dress to school every day and is teased by the 'in girls', who have many beautiful dresses. It's a quick read. It's a powerful story. Definitely a skinny-punch book.

Enough books for today. Time for a movie. I change into pyjamas, shut off my light and, as soon as my head hits the pillow, the summer matinee starts in my mind.

JFK and I biking along that sunny bike path, the wind whistling, boats bobbing in the water. He looks at me with those sea-blue eyes and kisses ice cream from my nose.

16

The Cape Cod Beach Boys

Art is a jealous mistress.

– Emerson

Wednesday sails by in a minute.

I visit Salty. Hurrah, still no owner.

Tina and Ruby are coming out of Cohen's card shop in town. Their 'book' is 'going to be a bestseller'!

'It's not all wordy like a lot of books,' Tina says. 'Just a little bio on each boy and a breakdown on where they like to take dates, their taste in music, just the important stuff.'

So far they've got twenty boys featured from four Cape towns and they're not stopping till they hit Provincetown. That's the final point on the Cape. After that they'd have to head out on to the Atlantic hunting for hunky fisherman. Which might actually not be a bad idea for a sequel.

'Wow, that sounds like a lot of work,' I say.

'The price one pays for art,' Ruby says, wiping her brow like she's been cleaning toilets all day. Tina giggles.

'Do you have a title yet?' I ask. Wait until I tell Mariel about this.

'The Beach Boys of Cape Cod,' Tina says.

'I like it,' I say.

'We're not sure about the price,' Ruby says. 'We're thinking fifty, sixty bucks.'

'For a book?' I say.

'Well it's words *and pictures*,' Tina says. 'And wait until you see these photographs. Ruby is a really good photographer. I mean this is going to be like the summer swimsuit issue of *Sports Illustrated*, except it's all boys. All buff and beautiful . . .'

'In bathing suits, right?' I say.

'Yes, Willa,' Tina rolls her eyes. The she whispers, 'Well, most of them anyway.' She and Ruby laugh. 'Just kidding.'

'Who's going to publish it?' I ask.

'Oh, Willa,' Ruby huffs, rolling her eyes. 'You're

such a Debbie Downer. Details, details. Leave it to you to worry about something.'

Tina looks at me like she feels bad. 'I haven't seen you around, Willa. Let's do something this weekend,' she says.

'I'm busy,' I say, and then I brighten up. 'Guess what? I'm doing a solo wedding on Saturday.'

'Your mother's letting you?' Ruby says. Ruby remembers how when I first moved to Bramble, Ruby's aunt was getting married and my mother wouldn't even let me near her wedding-planning studio.

'Yes,' I say. 'Mom and I are partners now.' I look at Tina. She smiles, but doesn't seem excited. I think of how thrilled she was when her favourite soap star was getting married and my mother was planning the wedding and Tina and I snuck into the reception. That seems like so long ago now.

'Let's go,' Ruby says. 'So many lifeguards, so little time.'

I watch them walk away.

I stop by Nana's to pick up candy for Nico and Sofia, lots and lots of it, and bike over to visit them like I promised.

Mr Sanchez is home today. He says he wants to talk with my mother about a quinceañera party at the inn for Mariel when she turns fifteen in August.

'Papa, no,' I hear Mare whisper, 'you know we can't afford—' But he puts his hand up to silence her.

My mother comes in all red and sweating from jogging when I get home.

'You're running late today,' I say. She usually runs first thing in the morning.

'I'm starting training for the Falmouth Road Race next month,' she says. 'It's always so hot, I want to get myself conditioned.'

'How long is it again?' I ask.

'Eleven k . . . seven miles,' she says, turning to leave. She swings back around. 'Hey, Willa, want to run it with me?'

I feel a surge of happiness. My mother hardly ever asks me to do anything with her. She's always so busy. 'Uh, sure, maybe,' I say. 'If I can. I've never run more than three or four miles, but—'

'I'll write up a training programme,' Mom says, all happy. 'You've got time. If you're serious, that is.'

'Sure, yes,' I say. 'Count me in.' I wonder whether Mom should be running so much so soon after losing the baby, but I'm sure she checked with her doctor. And I want to ask if she and Sam are planning on having another, but . . .

Mom grabs two water bottles from the fridge. She hands me one. I take it. 'Thanks.' This isn't the time to talk environmental issues, but maybe it's the time to . . . 'Mom, I went to the shelter to visit the dog today.'

She looks at me. Takes a long drink of water. Wipes sweat from her face. 'And . . . ?'

'And the owners still haven't shown up.'

'Well, I hope they do soon,' she says, finishing her water. 'Are you all set with everything for Sam's sister's wedding Saturday evening? I realize I've been so tied up with the Caldor event that I haven't even inquired.'

'Thanks,' I say. 'I'm good. I went over the menu with Rosie and checked over the ceremony stuff with Sam. It's going to be in the labyrinth, fingers crossed it doesn't rain. And I'm going to ask my friend Mariel if she'll—'

'Good,' Mom says. 'Sounds like you've thought of everything. I'm sorry, but I don't have time to—'

'I understand,' I say. 'On Saturday, you will be Wedding Planner One and I'll be Wedding Planner Two.'

Mom smiles at me, then looks at the clock. 'Oh, gosh, look at the time. I've got to shower. Willa, please do a dining-room check for me, will you? Make sure all the tables are set properly and that the girls used the new linens. Those old tablecloths were getting shabby.'

Well, at least she didn't say 'no' about adopting the dog again. I still have time to figure out a way to change her mind.

Up in my room I go online and search under 'water bottles', and tons of articles come up. I search 'Planet-Partners', and lo and behold there's a picture of the founder, Ruthie Gracemore. She looks like Sam's twin, only shorter and skinnier. The article talks about a new irrigation system they've just brought to three villages in Nicaragua. I search under the keywords 'polluted Ganges river', and up comes photos. One of a girl about my age. Her big brown eyes are bulging out of her face. Hollow-cheeked, she's just about to drink a skinny handful of water. *Don't do it.* I wish I could help her. I feel sad, hopeless, like, what can I do to help that girl, that particular girl right there in that photo? I wonder what her name is. I wonder how old she is. I wonder if she's gotten some fresh clean water by now.

Water, water, everywhere. I think of that day on the beach, how thirsty I was, how awful it would be to be really thirsty, actually dying from thirst.

Maybe I will find a way to raise money for Planet-Partners or for the organization Dr Swaminathan is connected with in India. I think of Dr Swammy's bumper sticker – *Think Global. Start Local.*

Tonight I choose *Missing May* by Cynthia Rylant. I first read it when I was in fourth grade, one of those books you come back to again. It's so hopeful. And I like the fact that the girl's name is Summer.

I write in my journal.

Only one more night until Ruthie arrives. Curious.

Only two more nights until Joseph leaves. Sad.

Only three more nights until my first solo wedding. Excited.

Only four more nights until Salty is mine. Hurrah!

17

Two Planets Colliding

There are persons both of superior character and
*   intellect*
Whose superiority quite disappears when they are
*   put together.*
They neutralize, anticipate, puzzle and belittle
*   each other.*

– Emerson

Mom and Sam are in the kitchen having coffee early Thursday morning before Rosie and the others arrive.

'Willa assures me she has everything under control for the wedding,' Mom says. 'Oh, and I'm putting them in the Norman Rockwell suite on the third floor.'

'That's a very nice room,' Sam says, 'thank you.'

'And you said you think they have six or seven friends coming,' Mom says. 'I'm assuming they expect to stay here. I'm saving the Whitman Lodge by the pond.'

'Great,' Sam says, 'thank you.'

'I've got a luncheon today,' Mom says, 'the Caldor rehearsal tomorrow, and then Saturday, as you know, I'll be completely tied up all day with the wedding and reception. All I'll have time to do is shower and show up in the labyrinth Saturday night at six.'

'Stella . . .' There's a long pause. 'I appreciate your willingness to bend a bit on this one.'

'What do you mean "bend a bit"?' There's an edge to my mother's voice.

'I just mean that I know how you like to run things, and this was sprung upon you at the last minute and—'

'Sam, honey,' Mom says. 'She's your *sister*. I'll deal with it.'

Way to go, Mom. I like the new bendable Stella. I think of that little green rubbery toy I had as a child. You could stretch and bend him every which way. What was that guy's name?

'Morning, Mom, morning, Dad.' I head to the corner area where we keep a small refrigerator, pantry and bread box for our family's special food things. Rosie, Makita, Daryl, all our employees are welcome to have the meals we serve guests at the Inn, but the stuff in this section is just for the family.

I open the bread box and reach for the chocolate-cherry muffin I stashed there yesterday. Mmm . . . yummm.

Sam stretches. 'I'm heading up to take a shower,' he says. 'A nice, long shower. Maybe the last one I'll take in peace this week.'

'What are you talking about?' Mom says.

'Oh, nothing,' Sam says, winking at me, 'just don't want to waste water.'

When Sam leaves, the phone rings. Mom answers it. 'Oh, yes, Ruthie, hello! This is Stella. Yes, me too. You're where? OK. I'll come pick you up. No, it's not a problem at all. I'll be there in a little over an hour. I'll come to the passenger pick-up zone. I drive a silver SUV.'

'Willa,' Mom says. 'I'm off to get Aunt Ruthie

and Spruce. They took an earlier flight. Don't tell
Sam. Let's surprise him.'

'Good for you, Mom.'

'What?' she says, cocking her head
suspiciously.

'Nothing. I mean that's nice of you.'

When Sam comes downstairs, he says he'll be
back in a bit and goes outside.

I look out the window and watch him walking
slowly through his labyrinth. When he reaches the
centre, he sits on the grey stone bench. He closes
his eyes. I look away. I leave him to his private
prayers.

I go get my wedding-planning book and bring
it down to the kitchen table to look over the plans
for Ruthie and Spruce's wedding. Ceremony,
set. Reception . . . Sam will set up tables on the
pavilion by the pond and I've ordered a marquee
just in case. Flowers . . . I have a feeling Ruthie
would want simple, so I'm going to make her a
bouquet myself from the flowers on our property
. . . puffy blue hydrangeas for her, and for the
centrepieces . . . simple daisies, cornflowers and

Queen Anne's lace. I love that name, Queen Anne's lace.

That reminds me of a funny story I read about the origin of wedding customs. Back in the 1500s, most couples got married in June, because they took their annual bath in May and still smelt pretty good in June. Just to be safe though, brides carried a bouquet of flowers to hide body odour. And that's where the custom of a wedding bouquet comes from.

Dinner, set. I went over the menu with Rosie yesterday. She told me all the ingredients she'll need and I made a shopping list.

Rosie will finish the cake Saturday morning along with the Caldor cake, and I'll add the charms to each. Music, I've hired the the 'Wedding Man'. Mother gave me his card. She said he's not very original, but he's punctual and cheap. He brings a stock supply of dance songs and takes requests. I'm not sure what Ruthie and Spruce will want for their 'first song', but Mr Manny, aka the Wedding Man, says he's got pretty much anything they might ask for.

Oh my gosh, I forgot to ask Mariel if she'll

sing at the ceremony. Must do that first thing this morning.

When Sam comes in he says he's off to get groceries.

'Oh, good,' I say. 'Can I come? I have a list for Ruthie's wedding dinner.'

'Sure,' Sam says. 'I'd appreciate the company. Shopping's a lonely sport.'

We drive to the Stop & Shop in Mashpee. It's early and the market is nearly empty. A few hours from now it will be packed. We each take a cart and split up. I've never shopped on my own before. This is fun. I start in the produce section since I have a lot of vegetables on my list. The tomatoes and basil are coming from Sam's garden, but I need garlic, shallots, asparagus, broccoli, red peppers and avocadoes, lots of them. Rosie says avocado is the vegetarian's cheese.

The pasta is next. There's an organic foods section. I figure that's what Ruthie would want. I find a nice wholewheat linguine pasta and put several boxes in my cart. Then I choose a bottle of olive oil.

Next, French bread for the bruschetta. It smells

so yummy in the bakery section. I use the silver tongs to take two cinnamon Danish pastries from the display case, one for me and one for Sam, and pop them in a little white bag.

Sam and I meet up at the checkout counter. Sam's cart is full. We bag the groceries in the yellow plastic Stop & Shop bags. 'Good thing we have two carts,' Sam says. We eat the pastries on the way home.

Mother's car is in the side driveway. Sam will be so surprised.

'Now the unloading,' Sam says. 'I don't know which I hate more, the shopping or the schlepping it home and unpacking.'

I take two yellow shopping bags in each hand, the stuff that needs to be refrigerated, and Sam takes three bags in each hand, and we head into the kitchen.

Mother moves towards us like a storm cloud.

'She's a monster,' Mother says. 'Why didn't you tell me she's a nutcase? I mean, do *you* know how much carbon dioxide an SUV emits each year? My hair's a rat's nest, because the air conditioning was a 'senseless waste of energy' and so we had to drive with the windows down. I offered them bottled water thinking they might be thirsty from their trip and you would have thought I was offering her hemlock.' We hear footsteps coming. Mother looks towards the doorway and lowers her voice. 'The nerve of her making me feel guilty in my own car, doing her a favour picking her and her treeman up from the airport—'

'Samuel!'

We turn and there's Aunt Ruthie. Short and skinny with dark brown hair and Sam's big blue eyes.

Sam sets down the grocery bags.

She comes towards him. They hug briefly. She taps his tummy. 'Chunking up a bit, are we? And this must be Willa, my wedding planner.'

Mother huffs audibly.

'Hello, Aunt Ruthie. Nice to meet you.' I attempt to hug her, but she shakes my hand instead.

'What's this, Sam,' Ruthie says, like sergeant at boot camp. I swear Sam clicks his heels and stands taller to attention.

Ruthie waves her hands over our yellow

grocery bags like she's discovered hidden enemy ammunition.

'Groceries,' Sam says quietly.

Duh, I think. Isn't that obvious?

'Tsk, tsk, tsk.' Ruthie makes a loud, disapproving clucking sound. 'Sam, Sam, Sam . . . what in the good goddess's name am I going to do with you? Where are your reusable hemp bags? Do you know how many millions of barrels of oil it takes to produce these awful, awful throwaway plastic bags? They end up on the bottom of oceans and lakes and kill the fish and—'

'*Excuse me*,' my mother says in her general's voice, then she composes herself and smiles sweetly, 'but we have groceries to put away and things to do, so may I suggest that we continue this conversation later?'

I run outside to get the rest of those awful, awful bags. Oh my gosh, Sam was right. Mother and Ruthie are like two planets colliding. I hope the rest of us can survive the explosion. Oh, please, no explosion. I don't want anything to spoil the wedding!

18

Wave Talk

If the sea teaches any lesson,
it thunders this through the throat of all its winds,
'That there is no knowledge that is not valuable.'

— **Emerson**

Sam says he's going to take Ruthie and Spruce on a little 'sightseeing jaunt'.

'Good. Drop her off at the ferry dock in Hyannis and buy her a one-way trip to Nantucket,' Mother whispers.

'Stella, I'm sorry,' Sam says. 'I should have warned you.'

Sam leaves and I help mother with last minute things for the Caldor rehearsal dinner tomorrow night. The doorbell rings. It's Mr Sivler, Ruby's father.

I hear him explaining to Mother how the Bramble Beach Association is filing a legal injunction against the Audubon Society, claiming the superiority of people and their pets over wild animals like the plovers.

He must be the person who wrote that awful message about serving the plovers piping hot with fries. I have half a mind to say something, but I have no proof.

Mr Sivler asks Mom to sign a petition. He gives her a flag, number 279. 'Bring this with you when your family is at Sandy Beach,' he says. 'This is how'll we identify property owners.'

'Does he think he owns the ocean too?' I say to Mom after Mr Sivler leaves. 'And what's he doing, going door to door like that? Running for mayor or something?'

Mom laughs. 'He's the president of the Bramble Beach Association and the BBA is just trying to protect our rights.'

'Well, I'm not using that flag,' I say. 'I think it's stupid. We don't own that sand. That beach was here a long time before we were, and those birds, well, I think we have an obligation to protect them.

So what if people are a little inconvenienced.'

'Now *you* sound like you're running for office,' Mom says.

'Maybe I will,' I say.

The Bramble Animal Shelter isn't open yet. I bike over to Mariel's to ask her if she'll sing at Ruthie's wedding.

'I'd be happy to,' she says. 'If I can. When is it?'

I give her the details. 'Do you know the song "Let It Be",' I say, 'by John Lennon?'

'Yes,' Mare says, smiling. 'I love that song. I sang it solo at my eighth grade graduation. My momma was so proud.' Her face brightens up. 'Guess what? She may be coming home!'

'Oh, that's wonderful, Mare.'

'Daddy is determined to have a quinceañera for me, and Momma says she wouldn't miss it for the world.'

'I'll look forward to meeting her.' I'm looking at my friend's face so happy and I'm smiling, but inside I'm thinking her mother just better not let her down.

*

I bike past the Bramble Library, then decide to pedal back and stop in.

Mrs Saperstone is in the children's department, staring out at the whale spoutin' fountain.

'Willa, hello! Come see the new benches and wild-flower garden we've added out in the courtyard.'

We walk outside. It's nice there. 'How did your talk go the other night?' I ask.

'Went well, I think,' she says with a smile. 'The group of ladies staying at your inn certainly seemed to enjoy themselves.'

'The Red Hats,' I say. 'They're fun.'

'Yes they are,' Mrs S says. 'I'm going to get one of those hats, maybe start a Bramble chapter.'

'Did Dr Swaminathan come to your talk?' I ask, picking up a penny from the ground and casually tossing it into the fountain.

Mrs Saperstone laughs. 'You are such a sweet girl.'

'What?' I say, innocently. 'What?'

'You don't fool me, Willa. Don't you think I realize who set Javid up to coming. All dressed in a smart striped poplin suit, with a box of my favourite chocolate cranberries no less.'

So Dr Swaminathan's first name is Javid. 'Listen,' I say, 'if you need a good wedding planner, give me a call. I don't have business cards yet, but you know how to reach me.'

'*Willa!*' Mrs Saperstone says in a shocked voice, looking around, laughing. 'We're a long way from the altar, but it sure is fun to be dating again.'

Now for a quick ride to the beach. A day I don't see the water, is like a day I don't read. Every day it's different. Every day I learn something new.

It's high tide and the waves are sweeping powerfully into shore. I listen as they talk to me. Things are changing, things are changing, pay attention, pay attention. I have an odd feeling something major is about to happen in my life.

When I get home, Sam is pulling into the parking lot. Aunt Ruthie gets out first. Sam introduces me to Spruce. He doesn't look like a pine tree at all. He's a tall, thin handsome man, Asian, with dark thoughtful eyes and a kind smile.

'Nice to meet you, Willa,' he says, reaching out to shake my hand. 'Thank you for planning our wedding. Ruth and I appreciate your efforts.'

'My pleasure,' I say. 'I hope you'll be happy.'

'Happy would be nice,' Spruce says quietly.

'No, Ruthie,' I hear Sam saying, sighing loudly like he's got a headache, which I imagine he probably has. 'I don't know what my carbon footprint is. Or Stella's either. But I think she wears a size seven shoe.'

'Not funny, Samuel,' Ruthie says. 'I've just found the first way we can trade. Let me go get my questionnaire upstairs and I'll start carbon-emission calculations on this household. It's nothing short of global ignorance not to know the extent of the damage you are doing to this planet, Samuel.'

I look at Spruce. He looks uncomfortable and his eyebrows are scrunched like he wishes Ruthie would be quiet.

'Right off the bat,' Ruthie says, 'there's a huge problem with having two large truck-sized vehicles in one tiny family of three. Haven't you heard of carpooling? Public transportation?'

I'm thinking Ruthie ought to be grateful that my mother drove all the way to Boston to pick her up this morning, but I keep my mouth closed.

Good time to get away. I bike over to visit Salty Dog.

Mr Sweeney says, 'Good news. Still no owner, yet.'

Thank you, thank you.

Now I just need to find a way to convince Stella to let me adopt him. Maybe if I offered to work extra shifts all summer. No, I already do my fair share for our family. Or maybe I could promise to keep Salty in my room and train him to stay away from the living room and dining room and all the good furniture. No, I have a feeling that dog has a mind of his own, used to roaming the wide open beach like he owns it. I doubt I'd be able to restrict him like that.

I stop by Sweet Bramble Books. Both sides of the store are packed with tourists – good. There's a new display of *Edward's Eyes* by Patricia MacLachlan. I loved her book *Sarah, Plain and Tall*. On the back jacket of the book is a photo of the author hugging a dog. The flap copy mentions Cape Cod. It's definitely a skinny-punch book. I have Dr Swaminathan ring it up for me with our family discount and I'm about to mention Mrs Saperstone, when Nana calls me from the candy side.

'Willa,' she says, 'come see! I started wrapping the taffy in tags last night and already people are noticing. And I had an idea of my own. I set up a little suggestion box, and listen to this. Some boy gave us a good one.' She holds up a paper to read:

Don't be daffy. Eat your taffy.

'He was very handsome, had an English accent. I thought about you, but—'

'I have a boyfriend, Nana.'

'I know, I know,' she says.

When I get home, I go to look for Aunt Ruthie.

She's standing outside, facing the labyrinth.

'Hi,' I say. 'Aunt Ruthie, do you have a few minutes to go over the wedding plans?'

She turns to me. She's crying.

'What's wrong?' I ask.

'I don't know if I can go through with this.' She lets out a sob, then turns and runs in to the inn.

Life sure is full of surprises.

19

Kindred Spirits After All

To believe your own thought,
to believe that what is true for you in your private
* heart*
is true for all men – that is genius.

– Emerson

I can't sleep that night. I want to help Aunt Ruthie, but I'm not sure how. Spruce seems nice, but I don't feel comfortable breaking the news to him that his fiancée may not want to get married!

The next morning, Sam is in his study writing. When he sees me in the doorway, he slides the yellow tablet into his desk. I tell him about Ruthie crying. Sam says he isn't quite sure what to do. 'I wish my mother was still alive,' he says.

Rosie shrugs her shoulders when I tell her. 'I think you need to leave her alone, Willa,' Rosie says. 'Give her some space. Everyone gets emotional before weddings.'

Given how busy Mom is and given how she and Ruthie seem to despise one another, I approach my mother as a last resort. When I tell her what happened, she looks at me for a moment and then her eyes begin to glisten. She smiles and says, 'Don't worry, Willa. I'll talk to her.'

What? I'm amazed. 'Thank you, Mom,' I say.

JFK calls, says he's leaving today. He's coming over at four to say goodbye. I start crying as soon as I get off the phone. I don't want him to go.

It's good that I'm getting the tears out now though. I don't want our last time together to be sad. *Stupid baseball.* I glance at the cover of *Edward's Eyes.* There's a boy holding a baseball glove looking so happy. I start reading. I'm finished in an hour. It's a beautiful story. JFK would like it.

I make a quick trip to Cohen's card shop and I'm waiting on the porch with a gift bag when JFK arrives. A cry catches in my throat, but I push it back down and smile a happy smile for him. He's carrying a paper bag with a shiny red gift bow stuck on. 'For you,' he says.

It's a reusable water bottle just like his.

'You said you wanted green, right?'

'Yes,' I say, laughing. 'Thank you.'

'I know it's not the kind of present girls like,' he says.

'It's perfect,' I say, 'I'll start using it today. And, besides, you already gave me the perfect present.' I show him the silver locket I wear every day.

'Still got my picture in there?' he says.

'Always,' I say. 'And here, this is for you.'

He unwraps the pocket-sized black-lined journal – Moleskine, it's called. Hemingway loved these. 'To catch your lyric ideas,' I say. The other gift is *Edward's Eyes*. 'It's about baseball and something more.'

He smiles. 'The good ones always are, huh?'

We go to Norma Jean's for ice cream. JFK promises to call. I tell him to have a great time in Florida. 'See ya in August,' he says.

Be brave, Willa, be brave. It's only for a month.

*

Mom says she had a good talk with Ruthie. She doesn't tell me details, just that Ruthie is a 'very strong-willed and independent woman', used to only focusing on herself and her work and she was getting last-minute cold feet about sharing her life with someone else. She loves Spruce very much. It's just that she loves her work too.

'I could relate,' Mom says.

I smile at my mother. 'Nothing wrong with being strong-willed, independent and happily married too,' I say. 'There's a way to be queen and not kill the king.'

Mom burst out laughing and hugs me. 'Who raised you to be so smart,' she says.

'Seems to me you and Aunt Ruthie are kindred spirits after all.'

'Maybe,' Mom says, 'but I'm not about to stop blow-drying my hair.'

We laugh. 'Mom . . . about the dog.'

Her happy face hardens. 'Please, Willa, stop. I'm sorry to disappoint you, but this isn't the time to bring home a dog.'

'When is the right time?'

'I don't know, Willa. It's something we would need to talk about and plan for. We just finished furnishing the inn and everything is just the way I like it.'

'But, Mom, I really, really want this dog. I love this dog.'

She sighs. 'Willa, it's a stray. It could be sick or—'

'He's fine, Mother. I've been visiting him every day and he's healthy and—'

'You've been visiting him every day? Oh, Willa. What am I going to do with you?'

'Let me adopt Salty?'

'*Salty?*' Mother starts to say something, then stops. 'Willa, I'm sorry. I've got to meet with the band leader for the Caldor's reception. I'll think about—'

'Oh, Mom, thank you.' I hug her tight.

'Wait, Willa. I'm not promising anything.'

'I know. I know. Just thank you!'

I run to my room and call Mariel.

She laughs and I hear Sofia and Nico laughing

in the background too. 'Why are you so surprised, Willa? I told you. That dog belongs to you.'

I'm so happy I could burst. Just a few more days and Salty's coming home!

Later, Mom knocks on my door. 'Willa, you wanted to come to the next staff meeting, right? Well, we're having one now, before the Caldors' rehearsal.'

Mother has name tags and a marker so that we can all learn each other's names. I listen respectfully as Mother, and then Sam, discuss their lists of issues. When the time is right, I ask if I may make a suggestion.

'Certainly,' Mom says. Sam nods encouragingly.

'I think we should adopt a no-water-bottle policy here at the inn.' I share the statistics JFK gave me about throwaway plastic water bottles and the information I learned from the Internet and the heartbreaking story about polluted water that Dr Swaminathan shared with me.

Sam shakes his head. 'Good idea, Willa. There are a lot of other things we can do like that. For a start I'll purchase reusable grocery bags the next time I go.'

Daryl says, 'I've been wanting to suggest that we offer guests the option of reusing towels and bedlinens, rather than washing all those towels and sheets every day. We waste so much water and energy.'

'I like that idea,' I say. 'I could write up little cards for the room explaining that we're trying to be more earth-friendly here at the Bramblebriar.'

A few other people make suggestions. Mother seems to be in agreement. This is good. We're starting small, but who knows where this will lead. I think of Dr Swammy's bumper sticker again: '*Think Global. Start Local.*' I feel proud that the Bramblebriar is going greener.

Someone coughs and I turn around. Aunt Ruthie is standing in the doorway with her arms folded, nodding her head and smiling. I bet she thinks she inspired all this. Well, that's fine by me.

20

Willa the Wedding Planner

The reward of a thing well done,
is to have done it.

— Emerson

Saturday morning dawns bright and beautiful. Rosie finishes the two wedding cakes and I carefully add the wishing-well charms. Mother is bustling about on top form, barking orders at everyone about the Caldor reception, and then she heads off to Bramble United Community for the ceremony. I wonder who the new minister will be tomorrow?

Sam is mowing the walkway in the labyrinth. The puffy blue hydrangea, sweet-smelling red and pink dianthuses, the roses and all the wildflowers too are flaunting their petals like bridesmaids' dresses swooshing back and forth on the dance floor.

I look up. Not a cloud in the sky. No need for a tent tonight.

Ruthie and Spruce's guests arrive and I escort them to the lodge. I talk with their friend Michael about the service. I explain to Ruthie and Spruce how the ceremony will go, the two of them, walking one, then the other, through the circle path of the labyrinth to the stone bench in the centre, where their guests and Sam and Mom and I will be waiting. Ruthie and Spruce asked Sam and Mom to be best man and maid of honour.

I see that the tables are set up on the pavilion, Twinkle-Lights strung around the borders. I pick daisies, cornflowers, brown-eyed Susans and Queen Anne's lace and arrange them in simple vases for centrepieces. I make a hydrangea bouquet for Ruthie and set it in water in a cool place in the kitchen. I double-check the menu with Rosie and leave notes for the staff members working tonight. I call the DJ. He's all set.

Then I remember something. All that time when Mother wouldn't let me help with the weddings,

I had a little secret ritual. Mother was known for her signature Twelve Perfect Ingredients for a happy wedding day. I would sneak down to her studio the night before the weddings and add a little ingredient of my own. I would sew a cherry pit into the hems of the wedding gowns. Just a symbol, really. A little seed of good luck and a reminder that the work of a happy marriage was just beginning. After the glow of the Cinderella ball, the perfect gown and food and music and flowers, from that day forward it's all about the love.

Quickly I bike to Nana's store. Good thing she has cherry cordials in the case.

When I get home, I offer to press Aunt Ruthie's wedding dress and she agrees. I take it to my room and carefully, very carefully sew in the Willa Havisham thirteenth secret ingredient. I close my eyes and make a wish for Aunt Ruthie and Spruce. 'And, PS, it would be nice to have some cousins.'

It's going to be a beautiful wedding.

Oh no, a *photographer*.

I completely forgot. Who can I get at such short notice?

A car passing by catches my eye and I look across the yard to No Mutts About It. There are bunches of gold and silver helium balloons waving in the breeze, and a large banner above the door: 'Grand Opening Today'. I run over.

Ruby and Tina are serving punch in the lobby. There are two silver-tiered serving trays with dog-bone-shaped cookies, one marked 'Poochies', the other marked 'Parents'.

'Hi, Willa,' Ruby says, offering me some punch. The door opens behind us and Ruby looks past me, her face lighting up at the sight of a fancily dressed lady with a tiny pinch-faced dog. 'Hello, Mrs Fieldstone,' Ruby says with a smile. She makes a little kissing sound with her lips as she looks at the dog. 'Hello, Fe-Fe. Such a pretty girl.'

There's a commotion behind us. 'Darling!' Mrs Sivler says, moving towards the doorway to hug a lady with two tall Dalmatian dogs. 'Welcome to No Mutts About It.'

'Ruby,' I say, 'I have a favour to ask you.'

'Sure, Willa, what?'

I tell her about the wedding and ask if she'd be willing to be our photographer. 'I saw what a great job you're doing with the lifeguards. I'm sorry for the short notice, but it's my first solo wedding and somehow I forgot about pictures.'

'Oh, that's right,' Tina shouts. 'It's your wedding-planning debut! Congratulations, sweetie. I'm so proud of you. I want to come see. Can I come too?'

'Sure,' I say, 'that would be great.'

This day couldn't be turning out better. I race to the shelter to see Salty.

Mr Sweeney looks up when I come in the door. I can tell by his face something's wrong.

'I'm sorry, Willa,' he says. 'The dog's owner came early this morning. He had the paperwork and tags and everything.'

'No,' I say, slumping down in a chair, my heart rushing up to my throat like I'm choking. 'Who are they? What took them so long? If they loved that dog they would have claimed him before now.'

'I'm sorry, Willa. I really hoped it would work out for you. But the owner is a very nice boy, a few years older than you, I'd say. He's not from around here. Sounded British to me. He was visiting friends on Martha's Vineyard and sailed his boat over, had it harboured off the Spit and the dog jumped overboard.'

Mr Sweeney talks some more, mentions other nice dogs and cats who would make 'lovely pets', but there is no substitute for Salty. I loved that dog. He was mine.

Heading back to the inn, I'm in no mood for a wedding. But this is Ruthie's day and I'm her wedding planner, so I push my sad feelings down deep inside and lock them up tight till later.

The inn is packed when I get home. My mother is waiting for me. The Caldor ceremony went smoothly and now the reception is well under way. My mother looks gorgeous in a pale blue linen suit. 'Willa,' she says, 'I've been thinking. And talking with Sam. I've decided to let you adopt that dog.'

A sob slips out and I dash upstairs before I scare all the cheerful wedding guests.

Ruthie and Spruce's wedding was perfect. The labyrinth felt holy and magical. Mariel sang like an angel. The bride and groom held hands and faced each other and spoke their vows to each other as if they were the only two people there. But we were there to witness their obvious deep love for one another. Ruthie and Spruce cried. Mom and Sam cried. I looked over and caught Tina's eye. She put her hands together as if she was clapping for me and then gave me a thumbs-up sign. I held my composure. I am a professional after all.

The dinner was delicious. The Wedding Man took requests and, because the party was small, everyone got one of the wedding-cake charms. Each corresponds to a letter in the name of our Inn:

B . . . a book

R . . . a rose

A . . . an angel

M . . . a mirror

B . . . a beach dune

L . . . a labyrinth

E . . . an envelope

B . . . a butterfly

R . . . a ring

I . . . an inkwell
A . . . an anchor
R . . . a rainbow

I let all the guests go ahead of me. There was one ribbon left.

The inkwell. I held the little charm in my hand and smiled.

'Which one did you get?' my mother asked.

I showed her. 'That's right,' she said. 'My daughter the writer.'

My eyes fill up.

'I'm so sorry about the dog,' she says.

'I know, Mom. Let's not talk about it right now.'

'Sure,' she says, 'I understand.' A song pumps up, an oldie about girls just wanting to have fun. 'Come on,' she says, 'let's dance.'

And for the first time ever, I dance with my mother.

She's a decent dancer for a mother.

21

A Startling Surprise on the Spit

I wish the days to be as centuries,
loaded, fragrant.

– Emerson

Surprise, surprise. Guess who gave the sermon at BUC this morning?

Sam. My wonderful father, the poet, writer and, most of all, great teacher, Sam Gracemore. Nana explained that while the BUC Board of Directors is searching for a new minister, they've asked certain members of the congregation to give the sermons. They are supposed to talk about their spiritual journey, what they 'believe'.

Sam talks about how he was raised in the 'Unitarian-Universalist tradition' and like the early leaders of this faith, Ralph Waldo Emerson and

Henry Thoreau, he finds his greatest connection to God in nature and, like Emerson, he believes in making time for solitude, for being totally quiet and alone so to listen to the voice within.

'Emerson said he believed that what was true in his heart was true for others as well.' Sam looks down at me from the pulpit and smiles. He continues talking. I look around the room. Everyone is paying attention. I'm so proud of you, Dad. I give him a little thumbs-up sign that only he can see, and he smiles at me and winks.

'In conclusion . . . I believe we are all connected . . . people, plants, animals. I believe that in our search for the divine we need look no further than the sound of the mourning dove, or the scent of the wild beach rose. We need look no further than into the eyes of the one seated next to us.'

I look at my mother and her eyes are brimming too.

After brunch, I change into comfortable clothes. I can't wait to get to the beach.

I rush down the steps, flip off my sandals, set off towards the Spit like I'm already prepping for the

Falmouth Road Race. Mom says official training starts tomorrow.

The beach is fairly empty. The forecast was rain. I keep running, the sand cool and soft beneath my feet.

Out at the end, the endangered-bird sign has been repainted. The ropes are intact. A tern scampers fast in front of me leaving little three-pronged prints in his wake.

Suddenly, I hear barking and then there he is . . .

'Salty!'

He's run-slipping, bounding over the dune to reach me, that great big smile on his face. I bend down and he lick, lick, licks my cheeks.

'Oh, Salty, I've missed you,' I laugh, ruffling his golden furry head. 'I love you, Salty Dog. I love you, I love you, I love you.'

'Willa!' No, it can't be.

I turn. Oh my gosh, yes it is. JFK is walking towards me.

'I thought you'd left,' I say, standing up to hug him.

'My flight was overbooked,' he says, smiling, nodding at Salty. 'I don't leave until tomorrow.' He squats down and rubs his hands over Salty's coat. 'Hey, boy,' he says. 'Good dog. You're a beauty. Almost as pretty as my girlfriend.'

I smile. Girlfriend. I like that. A wave of happiness sweeps over me. Then I remember he's still leaving tomorrow. The smile leaves my face.

JFK stands. 'Hey, you,' he says with a grin. 'You are my girlfriend, right?'

I smile and tilt my head down, looking at the sand.

JFK lifts my chin and pulls me in close.

Enjoy this, Willa, this moment, this now, don't worry about tomorrow. Everything you most want in the world is standing right in front of you.

JFK smiles with that dimple to die for and I sail away into those sea-blue eyes. Salty barks for attention, but he'll have to wait. I'm kissing my boyfriend now.

WILLA'S SKINNY-PUNCH
SUMMER PIX

Bronx Masquerade, Nikki Grimes
Edward's Eyes, Patricia MacLachlan
Esperanza Rising, Pam Muñoz Ryan
Green Angel, Alice Hoffman
The Hundred Dresses, Eleanor Estes
Locomotion, Jacqueline Woodson
Love That Dog, Sharon Creech
Missing May, Cynthia Rylant
True Believer, Virginia Euwer Wolff
The Whipping Boy, Sid Fleischman

Dear Reader

What books would you add? Maybe you'd like to start your own Pix List.
Happy reading!

☺ Coleen

Acknowledgements

With sincerest thanks to: my wonderful Scholastic Press editor Jennifer Rees for her excellent questions, suggestions and generous use of smiley faces; David Levithan and all Willa's friends at Scholastic Book Clubs and Fairs; my dear UK Macmillan editors Ruth Alltimes and Jane Casey, who cheer Willa on from 'across the pond'; my agents Tracey and Josh Adams; all the librarians, teachers and booksellers who introduce readers to my books; my mother Peg Spain Murtagh; my sons Christopher, Connor and Dylan; and, most especially, my loyal fans, who have grown to love Willa and JFK, Stella and Sam, Nana, Mum, Tina, Ruby, Mariel and the seaside town of Bramble, Cape Cod. Many of you have written to say that Willa is inspiring you to read the books on her 'Willa's Pix' lists, to start keeping journals and to write stories of your own. Whoo-hoo! That makes me (and Willa) so happy.

Read on. Write on. Dream BIG.

Till soon

☺ Coleen

Read how Willa's story began in . . .

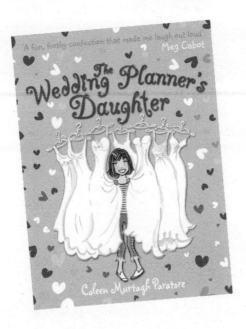

Willa Havisham nearly has it all: a sunny seaside home, a great best friend and her first ever crush. The only thing missing now is a dad . . .

For this Wedding Planner's Daughter, the work is never done. Now she's . . .

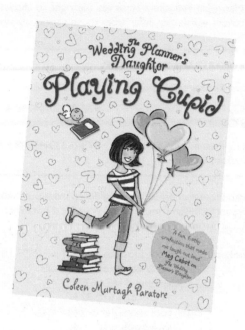

Willa Havisham has always believed in Cupid and the heart-thumping magic of true love. But just when it matters most, it looks like Cupid is about to let her down . . .

A selected list of titles available from Macmillan Children's Books

The prices shown below are correct at the time of going to press. However, Macmillan Publishers reserves the right to show new retail prices on covers, which may differ from those previously advertised.

COLEEN MURTAGH PARATORE

The Wedding Planner's Daughter	978-0-330-44297-8	£4.99
The Wedding Planner's Daughter: Playing Cupid	978-0-330-44298-5	£4.99
The Wedding Planner's Daughter: Star-Crossed Summer	978-0-330-45009-6	£4.99

All Pan Macmillan titles can be ordered from our website, www.panmacmillan.com, or from your local bookshop and are also available by post from:

Bookpost, PO Box 29, Douglas, Isle of Man IM99 1BQ
Credit cards accepted. For details:
Telephone: 01624 677237
Fax: 01624 670 923
Email: bookshop@enterprise.net
www.bookpost.co.uk

Free postage and packing in the United Kingdom